UPGRADED TO A REAL BOSS 2

BY

T. FRIDAY

Dedications

This book is dedicated to the five most important people in my life. My brat pack: Jordin, Jacob, Jacory, Jakayla, and Jalisa. Please understand that everything I do and every struggle I overcome is so you guys don't have to worry about a thing. I love you guys and don't ever forget it.

To my Blunt, you have been in my corner and stood by me for the last 15 years. Although I be getting on your nerves, you never switched up on me. Our bond is unbreakable.

Acknowledgements

To my publisher, Racquel Williams of RWP, you rock!!!! People always say make your first choice your best one, and I can say making you my first and only publisher was the best decision I could have ever made. Over the few years of working with you, I have learned so much in this industry. No matter what the situation is, you have had my back each and every way. You have shown me nothing but love and for that, I truly appreciate you.

To my Pen Sister, Christine Davis, it's because of you that I'm doing something I love. I really appreciate you and your grind.

To my wonderful readers and my supporters, I'm nothing without you guys. For the last 4 years and 25 books later, you guys have read and reviewed all of my books, and I appreciate each and every one of you guys. I really just want to say thank you from the bottom of my heart. It really touches my heart when I hear some of you say I have become one of your favorite authors. You all make me keep going stronger.

To my dearest baby sister, Amanda Jordin Hollis, my white chick, I love and miss you so much. I swear 15 years wasn't long enough to have you here with us. I'd give anything to hear your voice again.

To my mom, Lisa, and dad, David, I wish you guys were here to see that I'm finally doing something I love. I love and miss you guys so much. Please continue to watch over the family.

Previously in Upgraded to a Real Boss…

Two weeks later, Ms. Caldwell went to pay her son a visit. Like any other time, she didn't bring good news.

"Hey, Ma. What brings you here after ignoring me for so long?"

Shaking her head, she cut straight to the chase.

"Sunshine had the baby. Mya is finally here. I'm surprised she made it through all y'all bullshit."

Monsta smiled. "My baby, Mya Caldwell," he said with a big kool aid smile.

"They let you smoke dope in here, boy?"

"Fuck you talking about, Ma?" he questioned.

"Mya Bentley is finally here. Did you think that girl was gon' give that baby your last name?" she asked, laughing at her son.

Monsta jumped up. "You lyin'. Tell me that bitch didn't give my baby that nigga's last name."

The guard walked over to calm him down. "You gotta sit down, boy, or your visiting hour is over."

Monsta stood there in his feelings. "Get the fuck away from me, bro."

"Monsta, sit your ass down. You deserve this hurt for everything you did to that girl."

Monsta slammed his fist on the table. "Oh, you think this shit funny?

Fuck you, fuck Sunshine, that fuckin' baby and especially that nigga that was supposed to be dead! Fuck everybody!" Monsta yelled, picking up his chair and flinging it towards his mama.

She was grateful for the glass that divided them.

The guard grabbed him, and Monsta went crazy. Next thing Ms. Caldwell knew, more guards were jumping on her son. They pulled her out the building. She wanted him to hurt but never wanted nobody to lay hands on him. She drove off, once again blaming herself and her fucked up way of thinking for her son getting hurt.

Chapter 1

"I don't know what your problem is, boy, but you gotta learn to let all that hurt go and serve your time without going to the hole every time we let you out. What's wrong with you? What type of person wanna be in the hole for weeks and months at a time?"

"A muthafuka that just don't give a fuck," Monsta calmly said.

The guard shook his head, not understanding Monsta's way of thinking. "Maybe you can talk to someone about getting you some help," the guard suggested.

"Help me out by shutting the damn door before I fuck you up, bitch ass nigga."

The guard slid the door shut before walking away, confused about it all. He knew being locked up could be tough on someone, but Monsta had spent most of his time in the hole. Just four months ago, Monsta had received some bad news from the outside world and ever since then he spent the majority of his time in the hole. Whenever it was time for him to join the prison population, he would beat a prisoner's ass or jump on a guard just to go back to the hole. He took a few ass beatings from the guards, but nothing seemed to faze him because he stayed on his bullshit each and every time he was freed.

Monsta sat with his back on the cold wall. He was hurting deep down inside over the way Sunshine played him and gave his daughter Jonas' last name. For one, she really ain't even know that nigga like that. On top of that, the way his mother laughed at his pain tore him down even more on the inside. He had no other choice after that day but to take her off his visitors list and stop responding to her letters. He didn't give a fuck how she was gonna get by without his help. He had to wash his hands of her petty ass. That dark cold room and his thoughts were all he had left.

Monsta tossed and turned thinking about his Pops. It wasn't long before he felt his eyes getting too heavy to stay awake.

"Look at cha', son, just look at cha'. I left my legacy for you to keep our name in these streets. I'm not proud of what I see, Monsta. All I see is you running our name into the damn ground."

With tears in his eyes, Monsta replied, "I'm sorry, Pops. I'm sorry."

"Never be a sorry nigga, just do better," Big Monsta firmly said.

"I am, Pops. I promise I'm gonna do better."

Before vanishing, Big Monsta gave his son one last look, hoping he was helping him out.

"I died a fucking legend. Don't kill off our family name by being locked up for some bullshit. I taught you better than that. You get out this muthafucka and get your

bread and title back in these streets. Fuck all that other bullshit."

Monsta jumped up, reaching out, hoping he could at least get a hug from his Pops, but Big Monsta was gone. The whole situation had him in his feelings. He cried out for his Pops knowing he was the only one that truly understood him besides Sunshine.

The next morning Monsta thought back to what the guard and his Pops told him and decided to look into it. The first thing he had to do to get his plan popping is act like he had some fucking sense when he got released from the hole again in three weeks. Maybe it was time to admit he did in fact have problems so he could get the help he needed.

"Hey, my Mya Pie," Sunshine said as she played with Mya.

Ever since she had Mya, her smile never left her face. It was a blessing to have such a happy baby. Mya's face lit up every time she saw her mama and daddy. Sunshine knew what love felt like, but with Mya, it was something stronger than love. Mya had her whole heart.

Besides getting so much love from Mya, Sunshine also had to admit Jonas had been by her side every step of the way, and he was really a good help with Mya. When she was pregnant, he made so many promises. She had to admit that he was truly a man of his word. At first, she thought maybe they were moving too fast, but when the feelings are real on both ends, time didn't mean a thing.

Jonas stepped in the room fresh out of the shower.

"I thought you said you were putting her to bed."

"I am, baby," Sunshine said, still playing in Mya's face.

"You know all that keeps her wide awake and wanting to stay up longer," Jonas said, picking Mya up. He walked over to his side of the bed. "Hey daddy's princess."

Sunshine giggled. "And you were just talking about me. She got you wrapped around her finger."

"As she should. Y'all two know where my heart is. It's my job as her dad and your future husband to make sure y'all want for nothing," he replied.

Sunshine blushed. "Aww… You're such a sweetheart, baby, but I think you just wanted to take her from me to play. You not trying to put her to sleep either."

"I think you're right," he said, placing a kiss on May's cheek, causing her to giggle.

Since the birth of Mya, Jonas had stepped up as a great father and provider. Jonas made sure she and Mya never went without. He never knew about the money Sunshine stole from Monsta, but that still wouldn't have stopped him from being the provider in the home. He told Sunshine since day one that he would step up, and he did exactly that. Never in his life did he think he'd find a wife that came with drama, but he was glad he was able to look past it all because Sunshine and Mya had his heart completely.

Jonas laid Mya down on his chest as he got comfortable in the bed. She was tired and was ready for dreamland.

"How was your day?"

"It was going good until I bumped into Ms. Caldwell at the market."

Jonas sat up, damn near waking up Mya. "I know she didn't try any slick shit."

"Nah, baby, she didn't. It was weird. To my surprise, she acted like everything was all good between us."

"Really?"

Sunshine didn't say anything else, and her quietness alerted Jonas.

"Why do I feel like you're not telling me everything?" Jonas questioned.

They had only been together for a few months, but Jonas knew the look Sunshine gave when she wasn't being completely honest about everything. She had a cute telltale sign and didn't even know it. Sunshine looked down, somewhat not wanting to tell him everything. At the same time, she didn't want to lie to him either.

"Baby, we stood in the aisle and talked. She even played with Mya for a minute. She also told me she wanted to be a part of Mya's life."

Jonas wasn't feeling all that shit, but before he gave his opinion, he decided to see where her head was. "How do you feel about that? What did you tell her?"

Sunshine sat up, trying to choose her words carefully. "Honestly, I wouldn't mind her being in Mya's life. I told her I would talk to you first since you're her father now."

Jonas leaned over to give her a kiss. One thing he could admit is she's loyal to his position in their life.

"What makes her think it would be cool if all she gon' do is run to her son about everything? We haven't heard shit from that nigga in months, so let's leave it that way."

"She said she hasn't spoken to him either. Supposedly, he said fuck her, removed her from his visitors list and stopped responding to her letters. I told you that boy ain't all there in the head."

Jonas buried his head in his hands before looking back up at Sunshine. "So, what do you wanna do about this situation?"

"I don't know, baby. Would it be right to just say fuck her? I mean, whatever happened between me and Monsta wasn't her fault."

"Hell nah! Fuck her, him and whoever else out there played a role in me getting shot. I don't trust the bitch."

"Jonas!" Sunshine called out.

Jonas got out of bed with Mya. "Forget it. Just do whatever you wanna do, Sunshine. It's clear as hell this nigga still got a part of your heart and you desperately need him in your life. I guess I'm just the loyal good nigga sitting around, loving you like a dumbass."

"Why would you say that? Do you really believe that bullshit?" Sunshine yelled as he walked out the room.

After storming out of the bedroom, Jonas went into Mya's room to lay her down. Standing over Mya, he spoke softly to her. "You my baby, and I'm not about to let your mama fuck shit up dealing with those toxic muthafuckas."

Sunshine didn't mean to piss him off. She was only trying to be honest about the whole situation. Making her way downstairs, she saw Jonas lying on the couch. If he'd rather lay on the couch than sleep in the bed with her, they had a problem.

"Baby, please come back to bed. We need to talk about this."

"I'm good, go ahead and go to bed. Don't you have plans to go see your mama in the morning?" he replied.

Sunshine took a seat on the end of the couch.

"Forget all of that, Jonas. Can you just listen to me, please? Yes, we did move fast with our relationship, but you shouldn't have any doubt in your heart that I love you and only you. Why would you ever question your place with me?" she asked with tears rolling down her cheeks.

"Mya got a fucking daddy. My whole family love her and treats her no different from the other kids. What the fuck you need his family for? Where was these muthafuckas when he was beating yo' ass and making you cry every fuckin' day?"

"Jonas, baby, calm down. You ain't have to say all that. Besides, I told you she was there and, for the most part, stopped a lot of that bullshit from happening. You act like I'm talking about taking Mya to go see him while he's locked up."

Jonas turned his back to her. He was over the conversation.

"Go ahead and do what the fuck you wanna do, Sunshine. If you think she needs to have a relationship with that lady then it's clear a part of you still wants to have an attachment to him."

Sunshine sat there in her feelings and silently cried. She hated that he didn't understand how she felt. No, it wasn't about pleasing Monsta. It was about Mya knowing her family whether it was hers, Jonas, or even Monsta's family. With her way of thinking, she didn't see any wrong being done.

"Jonas, can we try to come to an understanding about this? I hate for us to go to bed mad at each other."

Jonas sat up. "I'm not mad. Go get some sleep."

Sunshine wasn't giving up that easy. "No, talk to me, Jonas."

"Look, I don't give a fuck about Monsta or his mama. You act like you forgot about him having someone shoot up this very house like a fucking month before you gave birth to Mya. I don't trust them muthafuckas. What more proof do you need to not trust them too?"

"Jonas, it wasn't her that was doing wrong, it was her fucking son."

"You can't trust her either, that's all I'm trying to say."

"And why do you say that?" she asked, confused by the statement.

Jonas sat up. "Why have you been riding around for months with a newborn and no fucking phone?"

Sunshine didn't respond. Instead, she sat there with her head hanging low. Jonas allowed her a second to get her thoughts together.

"I understand what you're saying about him, but what about her? I'm not asking you if he can be in Mya's life because she has you, and I know you're all the father she needs."

"And you don't think that lady wasn't the one giving him all your fuckin' information? How else did he find out where you stayed or your phone number every time you got a new number? Come on, Sunshine, use your fuckin' brain, and think about this shit."

"Really? Use my fucking brain? For your information, she didn't have my new information to give out."

Sunshine jumped up from the couch before storming upstairs. At this point, she was beyond hurt; she was pissed. She thought they could work shit out before bed, but he was just as stubborn as her.

As she climbed back into the bed, she couldn't help but to be in her feelings. Although their relationship did start off fast, Sunshine really did love Jonas. She just didn't like how he continued to say she still loved Monsta whenever they had a disagreement. She allowed Jonas to take over the relationship just to prove she loved him and only him. Running back to Monsta would make her the biggest fool ever.

Since Mya's birth, Jonas has played the role of a living father to Mya and a great fiancé to Sunshine. Having them around completed his whole life. Still, whenever Monsta's name is mentioned, he felt insecure. He never said anything to Sunshine, but there's always a look in her eyes that rubs him the wrong way when she talks about her ex. He hated to admit it, but it was there. For a while, he tried to ignore it. Still, every time they argued, he made sure to let her know she still wanted to be with Monsta. Sunshine denied it, but there had to be a reason why she still needed to be attached to his ass.

Jonas stood in the bedroom doorway listening to Sunshine cry herself to sleep. Something he never wanted to be responsible for. He also never thought he was the jealous type, but feeling like Monsta still held a piece of her heart fucked with him daily. Climbing into the bed, Jonas pulled Sunshine in closer towards him.

"I love you, and I'm sorry for trippin'," he whispered.

Sunshine stared into his eyes. "I love you too, Jonas. I just need you to trust and believe that it's only you I want to be with. The relationship I had with Monsta is in my past. You're my present and future. I'd never go back to him."

Jonas smiled as he placed a kiss on her lips.

"Damn, girl, you're telling me everything I wanna hear," he jokingly said.

"You're so silly, baby, but I'm serious about this. I want you to believe me when I say it's only you."

Sunshine and Jonas shared another passionate kiss before he flipped her on her back and positioned himself between her legs.

"I don't think I can do this shit," Keisha cried in the interrogation room.

The lead detective, Det. Marshall, was getting sick and tired of Keisha's shit. She needed her to pull herself out of that crying shit and help build the case that would bring Monsta and his family down for good. Growing up, Det. Marshall could remember hearing her dad speak so much about bringing this crime family down before he was killed in the line of duty. She now dedicated her whole career to bringing them down herself and making her father proud.

"Look, Keisha, this guy almost killed you and your unborn baby. You have to help us build this case and keep him locked up for good."

"I'm scared. Y'all can't protect me from him!" Keisha yelled.

"You've been alive these last few months, so what you're saying doesn't make any sense. We've been protecting you all this time. Now wipe them damn tears, and let's get this muthafucka together."

Keisha sat there crying and rubbing her stomach, wishing she'd never told on Monsta in the first place. She never thought they would talk her into being a star witness in bringing him down. If shit went left and Monsta found out she helped in any type of way, she knew it would be on her head, and there's nothing they could do about it. She was a dead man walking.

"So, he doesn't know I'm helping y'all build this case against him?"

"No, Keisha. Right now, he is only locked up for your assault. But if he gets out, there's no telling if he will fly off somewhere and get ghost. We need to keep him locked up while we get all our paperwork together."

Keisha sat there thinking things over. "What if I only wanted to get him in trouble for fighting me? I don't think I wanna help out with the other part. I don't wanna die behind this shit."

Det. Marshall slammed her hands on the table.

"He's already locked up because of you. Do you want him to get out in a few months and kill you for real or would you rather help us keep his ass locked up?"

"Calm down, just give her a minute to think," Det. Fisher finally said, not liking the way his partner was handling things. He understood how badly she wanted to take this family down, but he didn't want her to get out of character behind it all. The last thing he wanted for her is to get herself thrown off the case.

Keisha stood up.

"What are you doing?" Det. Marshall asked.

"I can't do this shit. I need to get the fuck away from Detroit before y'all get me killed."

"Sit your ass down! You're gonna help us or I'll fix it and you'll go down as an accomplice in all his bullshit."

"You can't do that!" Keisha yelled.

Det. Marshall jumped in Keisha's face. "Yes the fuck I can! Now sit your ass down so we can discuss how we're gonna take that muthafucka down."

Det. Fisher couldn't believe what he was witnessing. It wasn't much longer before he walked out of the room. He wanted no parts in the shady side of business.

Chapter 2

"Hey, Ma," Sunshine said, walking into her mom's house with Mya in her arms.

After so many threats from Monsta months ago, Sunshine used some of his money to move her mom and Zoey into a new house.

"Hey, Sunshine. Hand over my grand baby," she ordered, taking Mya out of her arms.

Sunshine took a seat on the love seat. "Ma, I need to talk to you about something."

Ms. Mathews took a seat on the couch. "What now, girl?"

"I think I'm fucking up so bad with Jonas. I'm scared I'm gonna lose him."

Not being able to control herself, Ms. Mathews laughed. "Girl, that man loves you and Mya. I'm willing to bet any amount of money he ain't going nowhere. You are overreacting and doing too much for me."

"Ma, can you really be sure of that?" Sunshine questioned.

Although Ms. Mathews didn't like to put her two cents in her daughter's business, the desperate look on Sunshine's face worried her. She knew her baby girl needed help. "What's going on, Sunshine? What did you do now?"

"We got into it last night. I told him I ran into Ms. Caldwell, and she wants to see Mya. He is against her knowing Monsta's family, but I think she should at least know her grandma. Ma, you always tell it like it is. Was I wrong?"

For the first time in a minute, Ms. Mathews was lost for words. She sat on the couch giving her crazy ass daughter the death stare. She couldn't believe how stupid she sounded. Then again, Sunshine had always been a fucking fool for Monsta.

"Ma, say something."

"Are you sure you ready for what I have to say?"

Knowing her mama could be a little too real at times, Sunshine still wanted her help. "I need help, Ma. I don't want him to leave me. Was I wrong?"

Shaking her head, Ms. Mathews chimed in on the situation. "You must be on dope or something. Ain't no fucking way you think it's alright for my grandbaby to be around that bitch. Truth be told, I still owe that hoe an ass whipping. For real, sometimes a stepfather can be more acceptable than the real family."

Sunshine didn't respond. She couldn't understand how or why she was the only one who saw no wrong in Mya getting to know her other grandma. No matter what she and Monsta went through in the past, she didn't want to hold that against her.

Ms. Mathews shook her head at her daughter.

"You finally got you a real man and stuck on fuckin'

stupid. Fuck Monsta and fuck his baldheaded ass mama. My granddaughter is not about to be in their muthafuckin' faces."

At this point, Sunshine was pissed off. It's her fault because she asked for advice knowing her mom had no chill and there was a chance, she wouldn't be able to handle it. Without saying a word, Sunshine jumped up from the couch, grabbed Mya from her mama's lap, and then stormed out the front door.

"It's a damn shame how quick your ass is to run away from the truth but took your damn time running away from Monsta and his bitch ass mama!" Ms. Mathews yelled as Sunshine walked out the door.

Sunshine bumped into Zoey as she rushed to get them in the car.

"Damn! Excuse you! I know you saw me!" Zoey yelled.

Sunshine didn't even bother to respond. At this point, she was beyond pissed, and Zoey was the best candidate to get her ass beat.

"Ma, what's wrong with your daughter?" Zoey asked, walking into the house.

"Jonas about to leave her stupid ass because she still wanna be in Monsta and his mama's face. Sike! Nah, she trying to get Mya to be around them people."

"Wow! Are you fucking serious? That girl loves learning the hard way. You would have thought Monsta knocked some sense into her ass," Zoey said, shaking her head.

"She's just as crazy as that nigga Monsta," Ms. Mathews mentioned.

Darryl stood in the doorway listening to them talk. It was always some bullshit with them. He really wasn't in the mood for all their drama when he knew he and Zoey had their own problems.

"What's up, Darryl?"

"What's up, Ma? How you doing?" he responded.

"I'm alright, just dealing with my crazy ass daughter, nothing new."

Darryl chuckled. "Yeah, I'm used to how things are with y'all."

Zoey said what she had to say about Sunshine's situation but was also in a fucked-up mood. She loved when she seemed to be the favorite one in her mama's eyes, but she knew if her mom was to find out the news she had learned, she would be the new topic of discussion. Earlier that week, Darryl had a job interview. They just found out he didn't get the job because he tested positive for drugs. Although wasn't shit funny about the situation, Zoey found it funny that Sunshine had been saying he was on drugs for the longest, and she never listened.

Soon as they made it to their bedroom, Zoey went off.

"So, how long have you been a fucking crack head, Darryl?"

Taking a seat on the bed, Darryl buried his head in his hands. "I'm not no fuckin' crack head. I told your ass in the fuckin' car that the test had to be wrong."

"Oh my gawd! So you really about to sit and lie to my fuckin' face, nigga. We have been living off my mama for the longest because you ain't been able to get a job. I thought it was just a case of bad luck when all along you been dropping dirty pee."

"I'm stressed out right now. I wish you would just shut the fuck up. You got too much fuckin' mouth."

Zoey continued to yell. "I just found out the father of my kids and the man I love is on drugs! How the fuck do you think I'm supposed to act? If, for a minute, you think I'm gonna be calm about this shit, you crazy as hell!"

Darryl knew he had fucked up, and his secret was no longer his secret. That was the main reason he hated when she wanted to tag along with him or be all in his business. Ain't nobody tell her ass to go through his emails to find out shit.

"Zoey, calm down, baby! It's not even that fuckin' serious!" he yelled, jumping up from the bed.

At this point, Zoey was in tears. "How can you say that when we can't even afford to get our own place? We've been living with my mom and she's been paying the bills and helping us take care of the kids. My little job at the restaurant ain't doing shit." Zoey cried as she paced the floor. "All this time I've been giving you money just so you can have some pocket change and you've been giving it to the dope man."

Not only was Darryl embarrassed, but he was tired of hearing the truth about his habit.

"Man, fuck you!" he yelled before storming out the door.

Zoey didn't bother to chase after him. On top of being embarrassed, she was hurt.

As Darryl sat in the car, he thought about his next move before he finally drove off. He had no intention of letting Zoey go, but he knew she needed time to process the information she had just learned.

Zoey was hurt as she laid across the bed crying her eyes out. It hit her that she wasn't sure if him being on drugs hurt her more than him begging her not to leave him.

Once Sunshine got home, she put Mya down for a nap. She only had a few hours before Jonas got home from the shop, and she wanted dinner done and the house nice and clean before he walked in the door. As she prepared dinner, she pictured Jonas walking in the door looking handsome as always and smelling good. She just knew she wouldn't be able to keep her hands off him. Although they were just together the night before, she felt like she hadn't been with him in a while, and her body missed his touch. Sunshine made up her mind that she was gonna do whatever Jonas thought was right. Although her mama pissed her off earlier that day, she decided to listen to her as well. There was an old saying that mother knew best.

After making plates and lighting candles, Sunshine waited patiently for her soon-to-be husband to walk into the door. She had plans to feed, bathe, and fuck him to sleep so he knew it was real and all about him. She never wanted him to question her love for him. Looking at the clock on the kitchen wall, Sunshine realized Jonas was running late. It was unlike him, but she figured maybe he had a few extra heads to cut.

Sunshine went into the bedroom to fetch the minute phone Jonas left in the drawer just in case of an emergency. She called him twice and each time, no answer.

"Man, what the fuck?" Sunshine mumbled as she received Jonas' voicemail again.

Being out of the norm, she panicked.

"Baby, you got me worried. If I don't hear from you in the next ten minutes, I'll be on my way to the shop to find you," Sunshine said to his voicemail.

Although she was dead serious and worried, she tried to do a little giggle at the end of the voicemail just in case she was tripping for no reason. She hated how bad her nerves were waiting on him to call back or pop up at the house. Sunshine took a seat at the table to start eating her food. Food always helped her calm down. Picking the phone up, Sunshine dialed Jonas' number again. Once again, there was no answer. This time, she didn't leave a voice message.

Later that night as she climbed in the bed, Sunshine couldn't help but to shake her head as she thought back to the night before. After their little disagreement blew over, they ended up making sweet love. She thought they'd made up. Seeing he didn't decide to come home or bother to respond to her numerous calls and text, she realized the night before was nothing more than a fuck. Sunshine prayed she was just overreacting as she cuddled up with Mya in her bed.

Jonas tried his best to get comfortable in his bed at his own apartment. He had been at Sunshine's house for so long that he couldn't fall asleep without holding her. Everything felt so different at his own place. He couldn't believe that he was ever truly happy being on his own before getting with Sunshine. On top of missing her soft body lying on his, he never missed a night of kissing Mya good night. His mind started to wonder if she was still up waiting on her daddy to tell her goodnight.

Jonas shook his head at the situation that had him torn. On one hand, he wanted to do whatever to make Sunshine and Mya happy. On the other hand, getting Monsta's people involved in Mya's life isn't something he wanted to do. He took on the responsibility to be in her life as her father. It was his job to protect her from any harm that came her way. He didn't understand how Sunshine doesn't see how crazy she was acting or thinking. She gave muthafuckas too many chances to prove to her they weren't shit, and he hated that about her.

As he laid across the bed, he picked the phone up only to place it back down. He wanted so badly to call her, but just the thought of her being on that dumb shit made him wanna give her some space. They both needed some space and a peace of mind.

Meka sat around listening to her cousins act a fool. At least three times out of the month, they tried to meet up for a family day. And just like any other gathering they were having a good time.

"Nakia, go check on the hamburger for those tacos!" Meka yelled out.

Nakia, lost in her thoughts, got up with no problem. Once she returned to the living room, she took her seat before looking down at the carpet. Family was everything to her, but things just weren't the same without having her brother there, enjoying life with them.

"What's up, Cuz?" Kyrie asked, noticing Nakia wasn't the life of the party that night.

Nakia looked up with tears in her eyes. "Shit's just not fair. I miss my big brother so much. My baby should be here with us, not buried in the fuckin' dirt."

Jayson killed his shot. "Yeah, somebody took a real nigga from us, but believe we on that nigga Monsta's ass."

"I know Trevor was family, but let that shit go. That nigga Monsta locked up and it ain't shit we can do to him now," Meka tried to explain.

"Meka shut the fuck up with that shit. Trevor was my fuckin' brother and you act like we not supposed to go after that nigga. The fuck you mean let that shit go?" Nakia snapped.

Meka snapped right back. "He locked up! If you ain't trying to be Ms. Big Bad Ass and bring that shit to his mama's house or whoever else, then shut the fuck up!"

Nakia jumped up. "Bitch you know I ain't never been scared. Fuck him and whoever!"

Mason stood up. "Y'all two, chill the fuck out. That nigga gon' get his, please believe that. I don't give a fuck how long we gotta wait, he gettin' his. I have a long life ahead of me and I'm gon' get my payback for my brother's death. Y'all better believe that."

As Nakia sat back down, she started to cry. "I hate that nigga so fucking much. He took my brother from me and that shit hurts every time I think about it."

Meka walked over to her cousin and gave her a hug.

"We family, and I'll forever have your back. I just want you to think smart about shit. Let them deal with that shit correctly. I don't want you out here trying to handle shit yourself and end up locked up somewhere."

"Hey, has anyone heard from Jonas? I thought he was gonna drop by for a little bit." Jayson asked, trying to change the subject.

"When we closed the shop earlier, he said he wasn't feeling too good and didn't know if he was gonna come this time around."

"I bet that bitch Sunshine got his head buried in her ass," Nakia said, taking another sip of her drink.

"Come on now, Nakia, don't start that bullshit. We all know he loves that girl. Besides, she's mad cool if you ask me," Meka said, taking up for Sunshine.

Nakia rolled her eyes. "Whatever. I just think it's funny how her baby daddy killed my fuckin' brother and y'all just invite her in the family like it wasn't shit. Since that bitch nigga Monsta locked up, I should just beat her ass every time I see the stupid bitch."

"Chill out, Cuz. Why don't you go lay your drunk ass down somewhere," Kyrie suggested.

Nakia was pissed that no one agreed with her.

"Fuck y'all. I'm about to go lay down, but when I get up, all y'all muthafuckas better be out of my house. And y'all better save me some fuckin' tacos."

As Nakia stumbled to her bedroom, everyone laughed at her except for Mason.

"Low key, I don't think she was playing. Y'all know how hurt she was when they found Trevor dead on the block," he warned his family.

Meka didn't want to think about Sunshine being an enemy, especially since she had lots of love for her and Mya. Besides, she knew Jonas would flip the fuck out if he knew anyone planned on laying hands on his soon-to-be wife.

Nakia laid across her bed. Yeah, she was buzzing, but she was dead serious about getting her revenge. If she couldn't touch Monsta, somebody was gonna pay.

Chapter 3

The next morning, Sunshine was in her feelings seeing Jonas never came home the night before. This was the first time since forever that he hadn't come home to her, and her feelings were hurt. She wasn't sure if he was still pissed off like she thought the night before or if he was somewhere hurt.

After feeding Mya and getting them dressed, Sunshine jumped in her car so she could pull up on Jonas at the shop. One thing's for sure, he would never miss work unless something was seriously wrong. Sunshine needed answers and she needed them now. She wasn't in the mood to be played with, and he needed to know that.

Sunshine took Mya out of the car and walked into the shop to find Meka setting up before they opened up for the day.

"Good morning," she said, trying not to sound so angry.

"Hey, Sunshine, what are you doing here so early?" Meka said, grabbing Mya from her arms.

"I was looking for Jonas. Has he got in yet?"

"Yeah, girl, he's in the office laying down. He must've had a long night," Meka said with a smirk on her face.

Sunshine didn't want her to think things weren't all good in their relationship. With a smile on her face, she walked off towards the office, leaving Meka with her own dirty thoughts about what happened between them the night before.

Hearing the door shut, Jonas jumped up. "What's up?" he said, rubbing his eyes.

"I don't know, you tell me, Mr. Bentley. I've been up all night waiting for you to show up. You didn't get any of my calls or texts?"

"Yeah, I got them," he admitted.

Sunshine slammed her hand down on the office desk. "So, let me get this straight. You got my calls and text and just decided to ignore me?"

"Yeah," Jonas honestly replied.

Although he was being honest, he was pissing her off. "What's the problem, Jonas? Or are you letting me know you're the type of guy who gonna be running in and out of my life? If so, keep the shit real 'cause me and Mya don't need that shit."

Jonas chuckled. "You being a little dramatic, don't you think? I do have my own spot and last night I decided to go home. What's wrong with that?"

Sunshine rolled her eyes as she smirked and took a seat at the desk. "I guess I'm doing too much. I was just worried about you last night. You've never not called or texted me back when I tried to reach you. With everything we've been through, you can't be doing shit like that, Jonas."

"I wasn't trying to scare you. I just needed some space to clear my mind. I wasn't feeling that whole situation with that boy's mama. That shit had me up all night thinking about keeping Mya safe. I even tried to look at things your way so we could come up with a solution, and I'm still not sure about this shit."

"Jonas, I was thinking about it too. At the end of the day, I really want us to be on the same page when it comes to Mya."

Jonas got honest with her. "To be honest, I never thought I would ever feel threatened by that nigga being in y'all life like this."

Sunshine gave him a strange look. "Jonas, you trippin', baby. He is my past for a reason. The years I shared with him could never compare to our months of loving each other. I really believe you are the one for me."

Jonas gave Sunshine a kiss. "Don't just think I'm the one. I want you to feel that deep in your heart. I know exactly how I feel about you."

Sunshine smiled. "I know we met for a reason, and you were able to look past the toxic shit that I was dealing with at the time. I love you so much for being there to save me and to make me realize what real love is."

Jonas held her in his arms before getting back to the situation at hand.

"Baby, you've been drinking this early?"

Jonas quickly lied then changed the subject. "Nah, that's not my style. Anyways, do you think she'll be safe with that lady?" he asked, although his mind was screaming hell no.

"Her son was the problem. I think Mya would be alright just dealing with her."

"How about we play it safe and just take Mya to see her for a minute before she really keeps her on her own?"

Sunshine smiled at the idea. "Thank you, baby. I think that would be a good idea. Then we could see how she acts with her and go off her behavior."

Jonas was glad their beef was over 'cause he couldn't picture sleeping alone at home again. Sunshine is his baby and the love he has for her and Mya is everything to him. After years of being alone and broken, Jonas could finally say he believed in love again. There was something about Sunshine that made him want her from the first time he saw her outside of his shop just months ago.

As he held her in his arms, he whispered in her ear.

"You know I love you and Mya, and I only want what's best for y'all."

"I love you so much too. I never want to sleep without you by my side again," she admitted.

Jonas placed a kiss on her lips. "Baby, I'm not going anywhere."

Just as they started to share another passionate kiss, Meka walked in with Mya. "I'm sorry to interrupt, Jonas, but there are like three people out there for you already."

Jonas grabbed Mya from Meka. "Alright, I'll be out there. Let me talk to my baby right quick."

Meka walked out so she could let the clients know he would be out soon.

"Hey, daddy's angel," he said, placing a kiss on Mya's cheek. She missed her daddy and told him by smiling.

Just seeing them so happy with each other also put a smile on Sunshine's face. She loved her little family and wouldn't trade it for nothing in the world. Jonas played with Mya for a few minutes before handing her over to Sunshine.

"I'm gonna get off early so we can spend some time together. It's Saturday, I'm pretty sure you can plan something for us to do."

"I'm kind of mad at my mom so she's not gonna want to watch Mya for us."

Jonas chuckled. "Don't say that. You know she will watch Mya, just say you don't wanna ask her."

"Well, you've been around long enough to know how we are with each other."

"I'll figure it out, just plan something out and have her bag packed. Now take my baby back home and get some rest so I can get to work."

Sunshine gave Jonas a kiss before they walked out of the office.

He recognized two of the clients waiting for him, but the other one had his head down in the newspaper. Sunshine was so busy trying to get out of the shop that she didn't notice one of Monsta's friends waiting to get his hair cut by Jonas.

"Welcome home, my nigga," Roc said as Monsta entered the cell they now shared.

"What up, nigga, when you get in this bitch?" Monsta asked one of his favorite cousins.

"Shid, nigga, I got in here about two days after you got your crazy ass in the hole. Why the fuck niggas tellin' me you been in this bitch wildin' out and shit?"

Monsta laughed. "I been on some bullshit, but maybe not enough. These stupid ass niggas in this bitch running they mouth about my fuckin' business."

Roc laughed. "Don't go looking for any more trouble in this bitch. My pops told me."

Monsta shook his head. "Uncle Rich talks to fuckin' much. So, what, he got you watching out for me now or something?"

"Hell nah. I'm just doing my time and getting out these white muthafuckas' faces. You can keep that bullshit up and these white pigs gon' make sure you do your time plus some."

After doing their little handshake, Monsta took a seat on his hard mattress. "I'm ready to get the fuck from out here too, nigga. I gotta plan, but I'ma need some strings pulled from the outside."

"Say no more, nigga. I got you."

Monsta spent the next hour telling his cousin about how he could work the system in his favor and be released early. Everything sounded so much better getting out of his head and into the atmosphere.

"Cuz, you know you have to stay out of trouble in order for that shit to work," Roc reminded him.

"For sure, my nigga. I think I can handle that for my freedom. I miss my girl and wanna finally meet my daughter."

Roc chuckled. "Cuz, I thought things were over between you and Sunshine. Word in the hood is you got Keisha's trick ass pregnant, and Sunshine done moved the fuck on with one of the Bentley Boyz."

"Fuck that nigga. Just wait, I'm gon' get my family back as soon as I get out of here."

Just the mention of Sunshine's name made Monsta forget about the conversation he had with his pops a few weeks ago.

Roc shook his head. He already knew the back story on Monsta and Sunshine's relationship and strongly believed she was better off without his crazy ass. Monsta didn't know how to love correctly and the last thing he needed is to be around her and that innocent baby girl.

"Cuz, you know she happy and engaged to that nigga, right?" he tried to warn him.

Monsta looked up so his cousin could see just how serious he was about getting his family back. "I don't give a fuck about what they think they got going on. I know for a fact she only acting like she want that nigga because she think Keisha's baby is mine. Sunshine knows I'm the right nigga for her."

Roc chuckled. "Yeah, ok, if you say so."

"You don't believe me, nigga?"

Roc could sense that Monsta was about to be on all bullshit, so he changed the subject.

"If you believe it, then hey, who am I to tell you anything different?"

"That's what the fuck I thought, bitch ass nigga. Ain't no nigga about to have my family while I'm alive and you best to believe that shit."

Jonas stepped out of the shower, ready to spend the rest of the day with his future wife. It had been a good three weeks since they last went out and just enjoyed themselves.

"Damn, sexy, maybe we should stay in today," Sunshine said, laying across the bed.

Jonas chuckled. "That sounds like a good plan, but I wanna get out of the house and talk. We can do whatever you want once we get back home."

"Alright, I'm down."

She could have gone for some long strokes before they left, but the way their bodies were set up, their plans of going out would've been canceled.

"So, who's gonna watch Mya tonight?"

"Nakia said she'll watch her. She usually didn't do the whole babysitting shit, but I told you my family loves her and Mya so much."

Sunshine was excited to hear the news. "I'm so grateful for you all. As you already know, my family's not close like that. Through it all, yours had my back no matter what."

Her words made Jonas blush a little. "We're all about family. I told you this when we first met. Now that you and Mya are my family, y'all their family too."

Sunshine loved his family's way of doing shit. For the most part, her family didn't really fuck with each other like that since their grandma died. She was the glue that once kept their family together.

"What's on your mind?" Jonas asked as he noticed her dazing off in her thoughts.

Sunshine lied. "Nothing, baby, I'm just ready to go."

"Alright, I'll be ready in a minute," Jonas said as he grabbed his wallet.

Sunshine laughed to herself as she thought back to Monsta having money in a shoe box and how Jonas had a wallet with cards and a healthy bank account. It wasn't all about the money, but she really had upgraded to a real boss.

After dropping Mya off with Nakia, Sunshine and Jonas stopped by the mall to pick up a few items. Sunshine thought they were just doing some random shopping, but Jonas had a plan he hadn't discussed with her yet.

"Look at this, I think it'll look cute on you."

Sunshine looked over the swimsuit he was holding. "It's cute but damn, that's a lot of money for something that's barely gonna cover my ass."

Jonas couldn't help but to laugh at her. She was silly but it really just told him what type of nigga she was used to fucking with. Since being together, he always had to remind her that prices didn't mean shit to him, especially when it came to her.

"Go ahead, get it, and stop tag watching. Stop acting like you don't deserve the best," he said, egging her on.

For the rest of their shopping trip, Sunshine didn't say much as Jonas picked out things he thought would look nice on her. Growing up in a house full of women helped him pick up on female style. Sunshine watched as he pulled out his card and swiped it without second guessing the total. Just thinking to herself, she finally found a real one. This wasn't the first time he took her shopping and spent money on her, but something in her was waiting for him to switch up. That's probably because of all the damage Monsta had done to her in the past.

"Where to now?"

Sunshine giggled. "Why are you asking me?"

"You were supposed to plan something, goofy ass."

Laughing, Sunshine yelled out, "Feed me!"

Jonas stopped at the red light. "You wanna eat for real or go home to get served this dick?"

"Both," she said as they both laughed.

"Your ass is something else, you know that, girl?"

Since the first time he took her to his favorite Mexican restaurant, Sunshine made sure whenever they went out, they ate there. Jonas learned to deal with her taco eating ass, but she made him hate their food.

"Baby, I'm not trying to be difficult, but let's grab this shit then go so I can get something else to eat. You got me hating this place."

"Alright, I'm cool with that," she said, laughing.

Sunshine sat in the car as he went into the BBQ restaurant to grab some ribs. Being caught up on social media, she never saw Kyrah sneaking up on her.

"Bitch!" she yelled as she opened the passenger side door then started swinging on Sunshine.

Luckily for Sunshine, she had taken her seatbelt off as soon as they pulled up to get Jonas' food. Because of that move, she wasn't trapped in her seat, getting her ass beat. She was able to fight back.

"Get the fuck off me, stupid bitch!"

Kyrah wasn't letting up and getting the best of Sunshine.

"Don't cry now, bitch! Your stupid ass got my brother killed!" Kyrah yelled as she continued to hit Sunshine in the face.

Jonas waited patiently for his ribs until a guy walked in laughing, "Aye, it's two bitches out there fighting and the yellow one gettin' tore the fuck up. That big girl tagging her ass."

Jonas grabbed his food as the lady called his name then rushed out of the restaurant. He had no reason to believe it was Sunshine fighting until he walked out and saw a crowd around his car.

"Get the fuck out my way!" he yelled as he pushed his way thru the crowd.

Finally making it to the passenger side of the car, he grabbed Kyrah off of Sunshine.

"Bitch, get your ass back!"

Kyrah tried to swing on Sunshine again, but Jonas wasn't having that shit. He wasn't the type to hit a female, but he was strong enough to hold her ass down.

"Get the fuck away from my car."

With tears in her eyes, Kyrah looked Jonas dead in his eyes. "This dirty bitch is the reason my brother is dead."

"I told you I didn't have shit to do with that!" Sunshine yelled, trying to defend herself.

Kyrah shook her head in disbelief that she was denying her part in it all. "We all know the truth, bitch. We know you were the one that took Monsta's money and set my brother up. How could you do that when Lamar was always there to stop Monsta from beating your ass? Bitch, I was there to pick you up when your ass was hiding in that vacant burnt up house, sneaking through the alley and shit."

Sunshine never really got into a lot of details when she talked to Jonas about what happened in her past. The look on his face told her he wasn't pleased with what he heard.

"Jonas, let's go."

"Every time I see you, bitch, I'm whooping that ass, and I put that on your daughter!" Kyrah yelled.

Sunshine tried to jump out of the car, but Jonas wouldn't let her. "Let that shit go."

The ride home was awkward. For one, Jonas was asking so many questions, and Sunshine wasn't trying to put out any answers.

"What money was she talking about, Sunshine?" he questioned.

"Just leave it alone, Jonas. Forget about that bullshit she was talking about."

Jonas shook his head. "I never ask too many questions about your past, but now I need you to tell me where it came from."

"It's my money, Jonas, that's all that matters. Now can we please drop the subject?"

"When we get home, I think we need to talk about this shit 'cause shit's not adding up."

Sunshine had an attitude. Him trying to investigate Kyrah's story pissed her off. It's bad enough she just got her ass beat, but now Jonas was looking at her all funny and shit.

"Look, we don't need to talk about shit that happened in my past. Just leave it there."

Jonas pulled into the driveway. "Look, if you took that nigga's money, this shit isn't just your problem anymore. Don't you think that shit has everything to do with why your ass is living like you in hiding now?"

Sunshine didn't say shit. She was fed up and embarrassed about everything.

"Open your mouth, Sunshine. Say something, dammit."

As she sat there crying, Jonas got pissed off. Her actions clearly were the reason for him coming after her. Her keeping it a secret all this time put him harm's way. For all he knew, Monsta probably thought he was living off his money too when he wasn't.

Jonas leaned over to kiss Sunshine. "Baby, I'm not trying to judge you or anything. I just need to know the truth so we can move around this shit."

"What do you not understand? I don't wanna talk about this shit, Jonas."

Jonas killed the engine. "We gotta talk about this, Sunshine. This the type of shit a nigga not gon' let die down. Not only is your life in danger, but so is Mya's. I thought shit was over, but hell nah. He wants that bread."

Sunshine opened her door. "Go get my baby then you can stay at your place tonight."

As she slammed the car door, Jonas jumped out of the car. "You're being real selfish right now, Sunshine."

"Go get my baby and leave me the fuck alone."

Jonas couldn't believe how she was talking to him. Since day one, he'd not only told her, but he showed her just how much he cared for her. Now it was fuck him just that quick.

"Leave you the fuck alone? That's really what you want?"

Sunshine never wanted him to leave her alone, but she wasn't ready to face the reality that she fucked up. If she didn't know shit else, she knew for a fact that if she talked shit and hurt his feelings, he would wanna get out her face. Jonas watched as Sunshine walked in the house and slammed the door.

"This shit can't be happening right now."

On his way to pick Mya up from Nakia, Jonas decided at the last minute that he wasn't about to take her back to Sunshine. Something told him she needed some time to clear her mind.

"Hey, Jonas, y'all on the way to pick Mya up?" Nakia asked as she stood on the porch.

After pinching her for the fourth time that evening, Mya wouldn't stop crying, and she didn't want Jonas to hear her over the phone.

"If it's alright with you, can you keep her until the morning?"

Nakia paused. With the way she felt about Monsta and Sunshine, she didn't trust herself not to fuck around and hurt or kill Mya's ass. Plus, she had started sipping.

"Damn, Cuz, my boo is supposed to be coming over tonight. You think she'll be alright with some ear plugs on?"

Jonas laughed and shook his head. "I'm on my way."

Going back to the locked bedroom where Mya was, Nakia started to feel bad. Mya sat in her car seat damn near sleep from all the crying. She was innocent in all this and Nakia had allowed the devil to take over her.

"I'm so sorry, Mya, I'm so sorry."

Getting her mind together, Nakia finally took Mya out of the car seat she had been in since being dropped off. She made sure to clean her off and change her dirty diaper before Jonas pulled up. Once she was done, she sat on the couch with Mya, feeding her a bottle. Mya kept her eyes on Nakia until she fell asleep. With that look alone, Nakia knew she didn't like her anymore.

Nakia cried her eyes out thinking about her brother Trevor. He'd always been there to take care of her and Mason when their dad ran off and their mom got sick. When he moved away to go to school and start his family, Jonas helped out as much as possible. It wasn't until Trevor dropped out of school and moved back to Detroit that they realized he was the one now in need of family help.

Trevor wanted to be on his feet before he brought his family to Detroit. Having too much pride and too ashamed to ask for help, he ran to the streets not knowing he was fucking around on one of Monsta's territories. Although Trevor was a good guy that made a bad decision, he didn't deserve to lose his life.

It was time Nakia realized that Mya and Sunshine had nothing to do with what a coward muthafucka decided to do.

"Damn, Trevor, why didn't you just ask for help? We had you, big bro," she cried.

Twenty minutes later, she heard the doorbell ring. Nakia wiped her eyes then got up to open the door for Jonas.

"What up, Cuz? How was the outing with your future wife?" she asked, trying to sound cheerful.

"It was alright," he lied.

Nakia gave out a fake smile. Jonas wasn't easily fooled and could tell she'd been crying.

"You good?"

"After playing then eating, Mya went to sleep, and my mind got to thinking about Trevor. I haven't seen his kids in a minute."

Jonas shook his head. "Let me know when you wanna go down there to see them. I got you."

"Thanks, Jonas. I really appreciate that, but Chrystal be trippin' like it's our fault he's gone."

"Damn, she still on that tip? The girl just doesn't know how bad his death hurt us. Our family is too close for anyone to ever think we would want to see one of our own dead."

Jonas picked Mya up from the couch to place her in her car seat.

"I really appreciate you watching her."

"We family. Ain't we supposed to have each other's back?"

"For sure," Jonas said, giving Nakia a hug before walking out to his car.

Jonas felt like it was only right to give Sunshine the space she needed and asked for so that night, he took Mya to his apartment.

"Bring me my daughter," Sunshine firmly said into the phone.

Jonas wiped the crust out of his eyes. "Sunshine, it's two something in the fucking morning, we sleep."

"I don't care what time it is, I want my baby."

Jonas shook his head at how petty she was being. "Look, just go back to sleep, and I'll bring her home in the morning. Is that alright with you?"

Sunshine still had an attitude. Although it wasn't because of Jonas, she still took it out on him. For months she held the truth about the money and now that he knew, she was afraid he wouldn't look at her the same anymore.

"Nah, it's not alright. I want my baby now," she demanded.

"Damn, baby, stop trippin'. What the fuck is your problem? Didn't I tell you she was asleep?" he yelled, waking Mya up.

"I hear her, Jonas. Bring my baby home before I call the police."

"Your ass is really trippin ' now. You gon' call the police on me because I have my daughter?"

"That's my daughter, Jonas, not yours."

Jonas wanted to hang up in her face for talking that dumb shit to him, but instead, he decided to put her ass in her place. "It's real fucked up how you would say that fucked up shit to me when I'm the muthafucka who always had y'all fuckin' back. You know what, Sunshine? If you want her, drive your ass over here and get her."

Being pissed off and embarrassed, Sunshine let those hurtful words come out her mouth and wished she could take them back as soon as they came out.

"I'm so sorry, Jonas. I'm so sorry, I didn't mean that."

"You said what the fuck you said and I said what the fuck I said. Come get her since she not mine. Now you can let her meet her real people without hearing my mouth. Ain't that what you wanted?"

Those words left his mouth, but he didn't mean any of it. Just the thought of Mya and Sunshine being out of his life was killing him.

After Jonas hung up on Sunshine, she immediately hated herself. Jonas was a good man and here she was, sabotaging her own relationship. As bad as she wanted to call him back to apologize and beg for forgiveness, Sunshine got dressed to go pick up her daughter. On the ride there, she thought about how Monsta used to always tell her she was so fucked up and damaged that if he was to ever let her go, none of her relationships would work. She never listened to that shit, but now she could understand exactly what he was saying. She was damaged goods.

Jonas opened the door for Sunshine after hearing the second knock.

"Jonas, I'm so sorry. I don't know why I even said that shit. You are her father and the only one she will ever know."

Something in Jonas wanted to forgive her because he loved her so much, but the damage was already done. She had broken him with those words.

"You can't be talking to me any kind of way 'cause the last nigga got you caught up in all this bullshit.

That nigga locked up while my dumb ass out here loving the fuck out of you and you clearly don't appreciate the shit."

"I'm sorry, Jonas. I swear it was a mistake."

"A mistake, Sunshine? Really? A fuckin' mistake is dialing the wrong number or something simple like that. That shit you just pulled wasn't a fuckin' mistake; it was your fuckin' truth."

The more Sunshine stood there crying, the harder it was for him to keep his guard up. His family was right about him being a sucker for her. This time she crossed a line he couldn't see himself forgetting.

"Here, it's late. Hurry up and get your daughter home," Jonas said as he handed Mya's car seat over.

Sunshine hesitated to grab the car seat. She couldn't believe how bad she fucked up with him.

"Jonas."

"What she needs to know is the truth. Ever since you bumped into that lady at the market, you've been on some real bullshit. It's like you're trying to push me away and out of your life. What the fuck happened, Sunshine? Did she tell you her son is coming home?" he questioned, pissing her off even more.

Jonas placed a kiss on Mya's forehead.

"I'm sorry your mama bat shit crazy and doesn't realize a good man when he standing in her face. I'm sorry I can't be your dad anymore."

"Jonas, baby, please forgive me. You know I didn't mean that. How many times do I have to apologize?" she begged.

"Do you know I just planned a surprise trip to Miami in a few days for our vacation? You just fucked up everything."

Sunshine was already embarrassed enough and that shit only fucked with her mental even more. She snatched the car seat from him then stormed out of the house.

"All this shit because she didn't wanna face her truth," Jonas said as he locked his door.

Sunshine sat in the car crying before she finally drove off. She wasn't sure how she was gonna fix shit with Jonas, but it needed to be done.

Chapter 4

"Let me get this right. After witnessing the terrible murder of your father, you were never able to get professional help from anyone?" Mrs. Howard asked Monsta as he laid on the leather couch across from her desk.

"No, ma'am. My mom actually said only white people seeked help and since we are black and from the ghetto, the folks around us would only tease me and make matters worse."

Monsta loved that they gave him a white, older psychiatrist. It was so easy to run game on her.

"Oh wow, you poor thing," she mumbled as she jotted some notes down in her notepad.

"Yes, ma'am. After his death, I was really fucked up in the head thinking that his killers were gonna come back for me. That's why I didn't like to be in the general population here. Every day I wake up, I have to pray for another day. I'm scared here, ma'am, to be honest."

"Yeah, looking at your file, I see that since you've been here, you've been in the hole most of your time here."

"That's the only way I know I won't be killed in here unless a guard decides to take me out. Ma'am, I don't mess with anybody. It seems like I'm being targeted because of the ghetto where I grew up. It wasn't my fault I was poor."

Mrs. Howard shook her head. She really felt like maybe Monsta deserved the help, and she could be the one to give him the right type of help.

"Mrs. Howard, I don't really like to fight these men here, but I just feel like if I'm angry all the time, I won't be messed with."

"Now, we've had three sessions already, and I do believe you have quite a few anger issues. The good news is if I can get you to take these medications regularly and behave, it might be able to help your case."

Monsta gave her a shy smile. "Thank you, ma'am. Nobody has ever tried to help me before."

"Now I have to run my plan by someone else, and it might take some time to get your medications. In the meantime, stay out of trouble."

"Yes, ma'am. I just pray no one messes with me."

For a whole hour straight, Monsta easily convinced her he only acted out when he was forced to. He told her he did have a few anger issues and when he did become angry, he hit people, but only because that's how he was raised. Growing up, he never received a hug when he cried for his dad. Instead, his mom used to punch him and call him a faggot for crying. Mrs. Howard soaked up everything and took her notes stating Monsta was a victim since birth and with the proper help and medication, he could possibly be helped from years of abuse.

On his way back to his cell, Monsta had a smirk on his face. He couldn't believe how easy it was to have his psychiatrist eating out of his hand in just a few weeks. Crazy thing is, while he thought he was getting down on the system, he was really about to get the help he truly needed.

"How shit go, nigga?" Roc asked as Monsta walked back in the cell.

Monsta looked down at Roc like he was crazy.

"How the fuck you think, nigga? Don't you see I'm in a good mood?"

Roc laughed. "Yeah, bro, it's as clear as day."

Monsta took a seat. "Anyways, did you get that for me?"

"Yeah, Amber came to see me today and brought that. I told you them white bitches love my black ass and will do whatever a nigga want. She also found that nigga Darryl for you and put him on game like you asked."

Monsta shook his head. "Good. I need my family waiting for me when I get out."

Roc didn't say shit else. He knew once Monsta had his mind made up, there was nothing anyone could say to make him change it. He spent so much time trying to convince Monsta to leave Sunshine alone and just let her be, but he wasn't letting her ass go for shit in the world. He wanted his girl and baby, and that was all to it.

Later that night, Monsta woke up in a cold sweat. Once again, he had spoken to his Pops and shit wasn't pretty. He accused him of still being a fuck up and chasing behind pussy instead of taking care of his business. Hearing what he believed was crying woke Roc out of his sleep.

"Aye, Cuz, you good down there?"

"Yeah, mind your fucking business!" Monsta snapped as he wiped his tears away.

He'll never let another nigga know he cried. That shit would make a nigga think he was soft and eventually try to test him. Little did he know, Roc had already heard him cry out for his pops before in his sleep, but never judged or told him what he heard.

"Ms. Freeman, open the door. It's Detective Marshall."

Today was supposed to be the day they linked up and discussed whatever news Keisha had for her. She thought she did her a favor by giving her time to think things over and realize she was doing the right thing. Detective Marshall banged on her door three more times.

"This is the very reason why I said we needed to watch this lil' bitch."

Detective Fisher shook his head at his partner in disbelief. "I told you from the jump this was a waste of time. You can't expect these folks to tell on someone they're scared of. You the fool for wanting his baby mama to help you out instead of doing your own work."

With that being said, Detective Fisher walked away.

"I'll be in the car."

Not wanting to believe Keisha had played her, Detective Marshall banged on her door again.

"Don't nobody live over there no more!" the guy next door to yelled out as he peeked through his door.

"Do you know how long ago she moved?"

"Nah, I really don't be in other people's business like that." With that being said, he shut his door.

Detective Marshall felt like shit. She had given Keisha time to calm down and get her thoughts together. She wanted her to realize she was doing the right thing while all along, Keisha had been plotting to get the fuck out of dodge. She never planned on helping them build a case against Monsta. Anyone that knew of Monster and his people knew he was not to be fucked with. Detective Marshall walked away feeling played.

Meka walked into the shop an hour early just like any other day and noticed the office door was open.

"So, you just gon' keep sleeping here like you don't have an apartment? Jonas, you actin' like a real life bum."

"I don't know why, but it's hard for me to sleep in my apartment or anywhere else. At least here, I know you'll wake me up for work."

Meka giggled. "You let that girl get the best of you, and I don't like it. And you're out of your mind if you think I'm about to let you work today when you've been drinking all night and probably this morning too. I'm gonna have Mason or somebody come get your ass. Snap out of this bullshit, Jonas."

"I did everything in my power to show her I was a real nigga and that I really love her and Mya," his words sluggishly came out.

Meka took a seat at the desk. For the last few weeks since he and Sunshine broke up, she'd been there keeping her cousin from jumping off the ledge. This wasn't the first time he crashed because a bitch broke his heart. The way she looked at it, he was too nice, and bitches loved them rude, disrespectful ass niggas.

Meka watched as her cousin could barely sit up from the couch. He was back to abusing the bottle and that shit crushed her, seeing as his dad lost his life years ago from drinking like a fish. Jonas had always been high on family and a child having a father because he grew up with an alcoholic father who died because he didn't know how to put the bottle down.

"Jonas, just lay down and chill until Mason gets here."

"I gotta open the shop, you know that, Meka."

"I got it, Jonas."

Jonas laid his head back down then closed his eyes. "What the fuck did I do wrong, Meka?"

"Nothing, Jonas. I told you from the jump she was gonna be trouble and came with a shit load of drama. You were a good dude for her. She'll learn that soon."

"I miss them so much, Meka. I can't go about my life living like they never were a part of it."

"Come on, Jonas. Just like you got over Nicole, you can get over Sunshine too," she tried to explain.

Jonas got loud. "You can't compare the two. Sunshine's just a little damaged and need extra love I wasn't giving her. And I learned Nicole is just a trifling bitch looking for a nigga to pay her way thru life. What me and Sunshine shared was real and everyone knew that."

Meka couldn't lie, the drunk did speak the truth. She hated how Sunshine played with his heart then spit him out like he wasn't shit. She also hated to admit her cousin needed Sunshine no matter what bullshit she was talking about. For the most part, she actually liked Sunshine and knew he loved her ass.

"Man, where that nigga at?" Mason yelled as he entered the shop.

Meka rushed out. "He's in here. Why don't y'all take him home and let him sleep this shit off."

Poppa shook his head. "We tired of his bullshit, Meka. He gotta stop letting these bitches get to him like this."

"Dog, shut the fuck up," Mason ordered.

Poppa was Jonas' little brother on his father's side. Jonas' Mom took him in when he was a teen because he was having problems at home. Poppa is the one who found their father dead. He hated witnessing his brother having another downfall over a bitch. He felt like Jonas was playing with his own life.

"Come on, Poppa, your brother needs you right now. He needs his family to have his back and get him back on track. I'm gonna make sure the shop is good while he takes some time off."

Poppa waked over to the couch. "This nigga act like we didn't grow up around this shit. We hated our daddy, especially when he was sloppy drunk in the morning. This nigga a whole fuckin' bum."

"Just help me get him to the car," Mason said as he walked over to the couch.

"Get the fuck up, bro! Get your ass up with this dumb shit!" Poppa yelled as they tried to pull Jonas up from the couch.

Meka could tell the sight of seeing his brother laid out looking just like their dad had him in his feelings. She understood his pain, especially since he was the one who found him dead.

"Poppa, I'm just gonna let him sleep the shit off," she said, digging in her purse.

"Here. Why don't y'all go get the donuts and stuff since we're about to open up."

Mason put the money in his pocket. "You sure?"

"Yeah, 'cause he's not getting up and there's no point in trying. We're gonna have a crowd in a few and everyone else will be showing up. Let's not give everyone a show."

"Come on, Poppa, let's go."

As they looked over to Poppa, he was sitting down with his face buried in his hands. They knew he was in his feelings and trying not to cry. They knew he needed some space. Mason didn't say anything as he walked out. Poppa and Jonas had a bond that only brothers could understand, and at that moment, Poppa prayed that he could get his brother clean again.

Mason didn't work at the shop but went to get whatever Meka asked for to make sure they opened up on time like always. They were all raised that family came first no matter what.

Jonas woke up looking around, somewhat feeling lost. Since Sunshine and he broke up, his new best friend was a bottle of Jack Daniels. Growing up, that was his dad's best friend as well.

"Damn, I need to stop drinking so fucking much," he mumbled.

Jonas got up to take a peek out of the office door and saw business doing good and Meka holding shit down like always. Feeling embarrassed, he wasn't ready to face his family with his new lifestyle. He snuck out the back door before anyone noticed he was even up.

Jonas sat in his car trying to think about his next move. If nothing else, the first thing he wanted to do is go home and shower. He had been drunk on his office couch and hadn't washed his ass in two days, so he smelled like he'd been soaking in liquor for a month straight. Looking in the mirror, Jonas hated who he was becoming again. He never wanted to be like his dad, but when life wasn't fair in his eyes, the bottle made him forget about what was bothering him in the first place. The only thing is when he finally sobered up, Sunshine was still heavy on his mind, which caused him to drink even more.

After taking care of his personal hygiene and another short nap, Jonas stopped by the phone shop to purchase a new phone before he made it to Sunshine's house. She had been avoiding his calls, and he needed to hear her voice again. He wasn't sure how shit would turn out, but he wasn't giving up without a fight. She had his heart, and he needed her to know it.

Sunshine jumped. "How did you get in?"

Jonas walked in the front door still a little buzzed but s o b e r enough to know how important this conversation was for him. He had the keys to the house but never wanted to just pop up after their breakup. Since she hadn't answered the minute phone, he decided this was the time to use them.

"Hey, I really needed to talk to you, Sunshine."

Sunshine picked Mya up then gave her the bottle she'd just warmed up for her.

"I'm busy, go away, Jonas."

Able to tell she was fronting like she didn't care about what they had, Jonas stopped all that. "Stop playing with me, Sunshine. You have no idea how this bullshit is affecting me. Can we talk as adults that love each other?"

"Jonas, I tried to apologize to you and explain that I said that bullshit out of anger. You're the one who wasn't trying to listen to me."

Jonas walked over to the couch and took a seat. Without saying anything else, Sunshine handed Mya over to him. "She misses you."

For the first time in almost a month, Jonas smiled.

"Hey, my Mya Pie. Daddy missed you, baby girl."

Sunshine grinned as she watched him plant kisses all over Mya's chubby cheeks, making her to giggle. Mya was nowhere in the talking stage, but her big, bright smile showed Jonas she wasn't lying about him being missed.

"I know we both have issues going on, and we probably need more time to heal before we move forward with everything, but I'm asking if it'll be alright if I can still at least be in her life while we work on fixing shit with us?"

"Jonas, you are her father, why wouldn't you be able to? I told you I was so upset that day that I said a lot of hurtful bullshit, but only for that reason. Mya is your child, and nobody can take the title as her father away from you."

Sunshine was happy to have Jonas there with her, but for some reason, the tears started and wouldn't stop rolling down her face. Jonas leaned over so he could hold her and Mya in his arms.

"It's gonna be alright."

"I'm a fuck up, Jonas. I'm so damaged," she cried in his arms.

He hated that she felt that way, but truthfully, they were both damaged in their own little way. Maybe the ones that thought that they were moving too fast in their relationship were right. Maybe they really didn't know each other well enough to be engaged and needed time to fix each other.

"Did you come over to make this break up official?" she finally asked.

Jonas took a pause as he thought about her question. He also wanted to choose his words carefully because he knew words could cut like a sword.

"Sunshine, you know I love the fuck out of you and would do whatever for you and Mya, but I think we might have jumped the gun a little. Lately, we've been arguing more than normal over bullshit that should've addressed early on in our relationship."

"Get out, Jonas! Get out!"

"No! We need to talk about this shit."

"Ain't shit to talk about. All this shit was fake. That's all I'm hearing from that shit you just said."

Jonas shook his head. "You know damn well that's not what I said, and I'm sorry if that's what you got from that. I just said we need time to get to know each other better before we get married. I fell for you quick as hell and put a rock on your finger within months. Won't shit fake about that."

Sunshine didn't say a word. The silence was killing Jonas. He finally got up from the couch and placed a kiss on Mya before laying her down next to Sunshine.

"I'll leave like you wanted. Just don't lie and say I never tried to fix shit."

"Jonas, wait!" Sunshine yelled out before he could open the front door.

"What?"

"I do love you. Everything about us feels so right, and maybe that's why we rushed because it was real from the jump. Yeah, some things have never been brought up or talked about, but I'm not ready for this to be over. Whatever needs to be worked on or discussed, let's do it. Just please don't leave me. I'm sorry, I'm sorry for everything," Sunshine cried out.

Hating to see her cry, Jonas rushed back over to the couch and pulled her into his arms.

"We're gonna work things out. You don't have to worry about me ever leaving you and Mya.

Sunshine cried her heart out as Jonas held her. Monsta had always made her cry. It made her hate him, and she always wanted him to go away. But with Jonas, she wanted them to be close and together forever. She wanted to be in his skin if that was possible.

"Why don't you see if your mom and sister can keep Mya for a week so we can take that vacation I spoke about before? I think we just need new scenery for a minute and to work on us."

Jonas walked in wanting to work on them, thinking maybe they just needed space and time. But the longer he held her, the more he hated thinking about space between them. He wanted his family back. Sunshine hadn't talked to her mom since the last time they got into it, and she really wasn't ready to talk to her or Zoey.

"That sounds like a good plan, but we're still not talking."

"How long has it been?"

"Whew, a long ass time. You know how we are with each other," she said, trying to play the hurt off.

Jonas shook his head. He went back to the old him that he hated when Sunshine wasn't in his life for a month. He couldn't understand how anyone that knew her could do without her being around for so long.

"Call them over, and I'll talk to them. You know your mom loves me and would never tell me no."

Sunshine knew he had a point. Her mom treated him like a God and it's been that way since day one. Then again, any nigga that wasn't Monsta probably would've gotten the same treatment.

"I can't call her, Jonas."

"Yes, you can, Sunshine. Be the bigger person and reach out. I had to be the bigger person and just pull up on you today because I wanted things to get back on track between us."

Sunshine had a dumb look on her face as she told him the truth. "Jonas, I wanted to call you, I really did. The only reason I didn't is because the night I picked Mya up from your house, I tossed the phone out the window."

"I thought you might still be that bullshit. I bought a new phone so at least Mya could Facetime me or something. I guess you need it now," he said, pulling the new phone out.

"Really? So, Mya was gonna Facetime you, Jonas?"

"Yeah," he responded, laughing.

Sunshine giggled. "I don't like us not being together. I feel so much better knowing when you get off work that you'll be walking through the door and embracing me with your love."

Jonas wanted so badly to tell her exactly how not having her in his life played a major impact on him relapsing and drinking, but he only told her how much he loved her. It was an embarrassing stage in his life that he needed to fight. "I missed my family too. I love y'all so much and never wanna be apart from y'all like that anymore. That month felt like a lifetime."

Sunshine felt like he was telling the truth and wanted nothing but the best for the both of them.

Opening up the box that held the new phone, Sunshine took it out then dialed her mama's phone number.

"Hey, Ma! What are you doing?"

Jonas sat there listening to Sunshine talk her mom into coming by the house to visit her and Mya. From the sound of the conversation, if Mya's name was never mentioned, she probably wouldn't have come. His family had their own problems so he couldn't judge. Mya played with Jonas until she tired herself out and fell asleep on him. That was a feeling he never wanted to give up. Like Sunshine said, he was the father, and no one could take that from him.

Sunshine got up so that she could straighten up before her mom got there. She knew she would talk shit if she saw how her house looked. Since she never told her mom that she and Jonas broke up, she knew she wouldn't understand that when she was depressed and stressed, cleaning up is the least of her problems.

Ms. Mathews told Sunshine she was out and about so it would take her a minute to swing by, but it was a whole two hours later when she arrived. Jonas laid Mya down on the couch so he could open the door for Ms. Mathews and Zoey.

"Hey," Jonas said as they walked in.

They both spoke as Sunshine walked into the living room.

"Hey, Ma. Hey, Zoey, where are the girls?"

"Girl, they're with their grandma like always. I swear it's like that lady doesn't know how to breathe without them."

They all laughed while walking into the dining room. Whenever they all got together at Sunshine's house, the dining room was the chill room. Sunshine wasted no time getting straight to the point.

"Speaking of kids with grandma, Ma, can you and Zoey keep Mya for about a week for me and Jonas?"

Jonas almost choked on his water at how she did that shit.

"Sunshine, I haven't heard from you in over a month and now you finally hit me up because you want me to fuckin' babysit? That's my grandbaby but you not about to use me, girl."

Sunshine rolled her eyes. "It's cool, you act like she ain't got another grandma. I was trying to be nice by asking you first."

Ms. Mathews shook her head. "Bitch, that shit doesn't work on me. Go ask that baldheaded hoe if she can babysit for your ass, but I bet you any amount of money if anything happens to my granddaughter, I'm coming for that ass."

"Ma, did you really just call me a bitch?" Sunshine asked, totally surprised.

"How else would you describe the way you acting? If you ask me, that was a straight up bitch move," Ms. Mathews said, justifying her choice of words.

Jonas didn't like what was going on and Zoey laughing only irritated him even more. He'll be damned if this shit led to Mya being at Monsta's mama's house by herself for a week.

"Ms. Mathews, I would really love and appreciate you both if Mya could stay with you two for a week. There's something me and Sunshine need to work out. We really need y'all right now."

Sunshine waited to see if her mom would go off and call him out on his bullshit, but then she remembered he got treated better than blood.

"She got clothes and diapers at my house. Call me when you need me to drop her off."

Ms. Mathews wanted to cuss Jonas out, but then she thought back to the last time she spoke to Sunshine. Her daughter was scared she was losing Jonas, so maybe they needed some alone time to get their relationship together. The last thing she wanted is for Sunshine to be lonely and broken. When her first real boyfriend and her broke up, she became needy and ended up with Monsta's crazy ass.

Sunshine peeped how her mama didn't even ask when or nothing. She was ready to leave with Mya right then. She fixed her mouth to say some slick shit but changed her mind. Besides, the look on Jonas' face told her she bet not fuck shit up. Instead, she went into the living room to grab the cell phone box.

"Jonas bought me a new phone. Take down my number just in case y'all need to call me."

Zoey and their mom typed her new phone number in their contacts.

"How long do you plan on having this phone?"

Sunshine giggled. "Forever."

Jonas smiled hearing that. Maybe her being scared was over with.

After they left, Jonas told Sunshine he needed to stay there with her. She was alright with that knowing she missed him fucking on her and just holding her while she slept. She never would have guessed he didn't wanna go home because his apartment was nasty and there were liquor bottles everywhere. Besides living in an unclean apartment, he didn't wanna go home to be tempted to drink like that again. With Sunshine and Mya in his life, he never wanted her to know the true him.

"What do you want, Darryl?" Zoey asked, wiping the sleep out of her eyes then looking at the big red numbers on her clock that read 2:47am.

Darryl hadn't been able to talk to Zoey in a few weeks since she found out about his drug habit. It surprised him that she even answered the phone. He had been sitting in the driveway for the last hour trying to figure out how he was going to convince her to overlook his habit and take him back. His little secret fucked up their relationship majorly, but the way he looked at things, he had a lot more going on.

"Can you come outside to talk to me?" he asked, somewhat begging.

Zoey couldn't believe he had the nerve to ask her that. "No! We don't have shit to talk about. I talked to your mom earlier and the kids are good!" Zoey snapped.

"Please, baby. Besides, I'm already outside and need to talk to you badly," he pleaded.

Zoey held the phone in silence. She wanted to hang up and hate him in peace, but her love for him wouldn't allow her to be great.

"Zoey, baby, I need you. You are my only reason for living. I'm not shit without you in my life."

Those words rolled off his tongue so easily. He'd never been able to lie so well. After seeing the money that was deposited into his account earlier that day from Monsta, he knew he had to do whatever to make Monsta happy in order to keep the money flowing. Darryl fell out of love with Zoey over a year ago, but instead of leaving, he stayed. Who wouldn't want to live somewhere rent free? On top of that, he was added to Monsta's payroll and could just blow his money on whatever.

Zoey wanted to tell him her house wasn't the spot and that's where he needed to be. She also wanted to tell him to go to hell. But being stupid in love, she climbed out of bed, making sure not to wake Mya.

As soon as she got outside, Darryl was all over her. "Damn, I missed you so much, baby."

Zoey broke loose from Darryl. "What do we need to talk about?"

"Come get in the car and talk to me," he ordered as he opened the passenger side door.

Zoey got into the car, no longer putting up a fight. Something in her wanted to hear what he had to say. She wanted to hear that he was off that shit and wanted only her.

Trying to play it smooth, Darryl lifted Zoey's face up so he could look into her eyes.

"Look, since you found out about my little problem and kicked me out, I've been getting my shit together. Having you and my kids in my life is way more important than having that nose candy," he tried to explain.

Zoey ate up everything he said and was quick to forgive him for everything. "Darryl, can you promise that you're truly done with this shit? I can't have that type of shit around the kids."

"I promise, baby, all that shit is over with. That shit wasn't nothing for real. That shit's out of my system."

Zoey leaned over to give him a kiss and show some love. "I believe you, baby. I believe you."

They talked for a while before Zoey realized she'd left Mya all by herself. "Me and mama babysitting for Sunshine and Jonas. I need to go in and check on Mya."

"Can I come in?"

Zoey smiled. "Yeah, baby. I'll just take her upstairs to my mama's room for the night."

As they got out of the car and walked towards the house, Darryl smiled at how easy it was to pull her back in. She and her sister were one in the same.

Zoey did as she said she would and took Mya to her mom's bedroom so she could have some quality time with her man. Determined to get his money while Zoey was upstairs, Darryl made it his business to snoop around. He made love to Zoey that night and made her feel like nothing in the world could come between them ever again. Happy to finally have her man back, Zoey took that good dick and was knocked out sleep in no time.

Darryl was usually ready to slide back into the wet pussy he once loved but being on a mission that was gonna make him money and keep him supplied with the purest dope in Detroit, he let her ass stay asleep. Creeping out of the bed, Darryl snuck over to her nightstand. If he wanted to get paid, he had to bring Monsta anything on Sunshine.

Learning that Mya was there is just a bonus. He knew a few photos of her would be worth a lot of bread.

"Got it," he mumbled as he strolled through Zoey's phone and found Sunshine's number. He couldn't believe she even had a phone. *Bitch must have thought shit was sweet and over with.*

Zoey flipped over. "What are you doing out of bed, baby?"

Before turning to face Zoey, he held the phone closer to his chest so she couldn't see the light coming from her phone. "I was about to go to the bathroom. Go back to sleep, baby."

Zoey turned around and drifted off, not knowing what she just allowed to happen.

Chapter 5

"Don't get me wrong, I love Jonas with everything in me, but I'm really starting to not like Sunshine. That bitch had my cousin's head all fucked up and shit!" Nakia yelled out as she took another sip of her drink.

Meka shook her head. "Here you go with this shit again. Sunshine ain't did shit wrong. If anything, she's the one who got him out that dark hole he dug himself in."

It was cousin night and once again, Nakia was buzzing and talking shit like she did every time they got together. Lately, her main focus had been on her hate for Sunshine, and everyone was sick and tired of hearing about the shit.

"Nakia, stop speaking on my brother. At least he got off the couch at the shop and he's trying to get back on track," Poppa said.

Nakia wasn't holding her tongue for no one. "I'm just saying that bitch pussy ain't made of gold. One minute he's living like a real boss, then the next, he acting like a fuckin' drunk on the streets. Why would he wanna throw away everything he worked so hard for to be like his fuckin' daddy?"

"Bitch, lay off my fuckin' daddy! I hated seeing my brother drunk and passed out looking like him, but you ain't about to sit up and talk shit about either one of them!" Poppa yelled.

Everyone there knew the back story of Poppa and Jonas' dad. They could feel the pain Poppa felt when Jonas was out there fucking up again. Everyone had sympathy, but for some reason, Nakia called the whole thing bullshit and blamed Sunshine for everything.

"You mad and in your fucking feelings, so I'ma let that bitch word slide. Anyways… I'm just saying, he acts like that bitch pussy made of gold or something. She brought her funky ass back in his life and boom! He don't need a drink and he's able to go on a fucking vacation. He ain't even thinking about the shop."

"Shut up, Nakia. As long as he's trying to get clean and stay that way, what's the fucking problem? You really need to stop drinking too!" Meka yelled.

"Bitch, whatever. We all drinkin' on something in this bitch, fuck you talking 'bout?"

Meka loved and understood Jonas so much. She wasn't up for Nakia's shit.

Meka put her glass down. "We sip on cousin night. You drink to get pissy drunk at least four days out of the week. We are not the same."

Nakia rolled her eyes. "So, what are you trying to say? I'm gon' end up like my uncle?"

Poppa didn't like that his dad's name kept being brought up. "You need to chill the fuck out. I asked nicely the first time. What my pops did is in the past and you out of all people not about to dog him or my brother out."

Nakia looked at Poppa like he was crazy. "I'm just speaking facts. Your brother is weak as hell for letting a bitch make him relapse again. He just showed us that if he don't have pussy, he's gonna slowly kill himself like his…"

"Chill out, Nakia!" Mason yelled, cutting her off.

Mason and everyone else could see Poppa was ready to fuck her up. In the blink of an eye, Poppa slapped Nakia's glass out of her hand and choked her up on the wall.

"Let me go, Poppa."

"Nah, bitch, this what you wanted. I asked your ass nicely to shut the fuck up about my daddy and brother, but you always want to push a nigga's buttons and shit."

Mason understood why Poppa was mad, but Nakia is his sister.

"Come on, Poppa, let her go."

Poppa slowly released his drunk cousin. "I'm gonna call it a night. I'll get back with y'all in a minute."

Although Nakia needed her ass beat for that bullshit she was on, nobody actually let him do it.

"Nakia, that shit wasn't cool at all. You know how hard they took their father's death and you sat in his face actin' like you were talking about a fucking movie or something. You need to go lay your ass down or something," Meka said with much attitude.

"Fuck y'all! For a matter of fact, y'all can get out my fucking house. This cousin's bullshit is over."

Mason hated the way she acted when she was drunk. "Nakia, chill the fuck out. Just admit you were dead wrong."

Nakia necked the last of her drink before slamming her glass on the coffee table. "It's time for all y'all Sunshine fans to get the hell out of my house. She got Jonas' head all fucked up and y'all allowed it to happen just like y'all let her baby daddy kill my brother. Now Poppa wanna lay hands on me 'cause he probably heard her talk about when she was getting her ass beat all the time."

"Chill out, Nakia. Everything ain't that girl's fault."

At this point, everyone was tired of her shit.

"Baby, it's so beautiful out here. This view makes me never wanna go back to Detroit."

Jonas was all smiles seeing his woman so happy. "Really? I'm glad you're having a great time. You sitting here talking about never going back to Detroit, but what about Mya?" he asked with a smirk on his face.

Sunshine giggled. "I'll stay here while you go get my baby."

Although she was very grateful to be on vacation, she was still clingy when it came to Mya.

She grabbed the bottle of wine that set on the balcony table. "Baby, you want a glass?"

Trying to overcome his secret addiction, Jonas turned the offer down. He knew that anything, including wine, would be bad. Especially if he was trying to quit cold turkey.

"I'm good, baby. The last thing I wanna do is get drunk and forget how beautiful you look in the Miami sun. That Detroit bullshit ass sun doesn't do you justice."

Sunshine blushed. "Aww, that's so sweet, baby. I love you so much."

"I love you too, and I promise I'm gonna show it every day."

For the next few days, Sunshine and Jonas had the time of their life. Being away from home made Sunshine realize she wasn't living life to the fullest like she should've been. Being with Monsta, she got clothes, shoes, purses and little shit like that. However, with a real boss like Jonas, he slowly showed her a better life.

"Babe, it's our last day here. What do you wanna do today?" Sunshine asked as she walked into the room.

Jonas stood up from the bed, putting his drawls on.

"Let's get married."

"What?" Sunshine asked, surprised.

"You heard me. Let's get married. Why wait any longer when we can do that shit today?"

Sunshine was all smiles. "Baby, are you sure this is what you wanna do? I mean, we were just talking about taking time to get to know each other better and stuff like that. Now you're talking about getting married."

Jonas grabbed Sunshine's waist so he could hold on to his love. "Do you love me?"

"Yeah, I do, but you said it was some shit we needed to discuss and-"

Jonas wasn't trying to hear what she was talking about. He couldn't see himself moving on without her and talking about his truth just might run her away. He couldn't chance it.

"Fuck all that! We're in love and don't wanna be with anybody else, right?"

Sunshine smiled feeling that his love was genuine and they could actually make this work. "It's a plan, baby."

His heart told him they were making the right decision, and there was nothing anyone could tell her about being in love. Sunshine wrapped her legs around Jonas.

"I'm so ready to be Mrs. Bentley."

"That shit sound sexy as fuck."

Jonas knew Sunshine was the one and would be open to marrying him at the drop of a dime. He also knew some of his family might have tried to convince him to wait, so he didn't plan on speaking about it until after everything was said and done.

Their last night on vacation, they spent the day as Mr. and Mrs. Bentley. They were happy and in love without a care in the world.

"Wake up, my beautiful wife," Jonas said, shaking Sunshine's leg as they pulled up to their home.

Sunshine slowly opened her eyes and peeked around. The car radio said it was past 12am, and she was dead tired.

"I'm up, baby. Let's hurry up and get into the house so I can climb in bed."

Jonas grabbed their luggage. He was all for them going straight to bed because he was dead tired too.

Jonas set the luggage on the porch then opened the door for his new wife, so she could go in while he went to get the rest of the stuff out the trunk.

"Oh my God, Jonas!" Sunshine screamed.

Turning the living room light on, Sunshine was hit with a major surprise. It had been a minute, but once again, someone vandalized her home. Hearing her scream, Jonas was alarmed and quickly dropped the luggage in the yard as he ran into the house. The newlyweds stood in the living room surprised at all the damage that was done to the home while they were out.

"Damn, man! What the fuck! Who the fuck did this shit?" Jonas asked, knowing neither one of them really knew the answer.

"Calm down, Jonas. Let's just clean this shit up."

Jonas gave his wife a strange look. He could sense she was hiding something.

"Somebody fucked the house up and all you can say is let's clean it up?"

Sunshine instantly caught an attitude. "What more was I supposed to say, Jonas? I'm tired and really just wanna go to bed so I can get my baby in the morning."

"Was it that nigga Monsta who did this shit?" he yelled grabbing her.

"Let me go! How am I supposed to know? Wasn't I with you?"

Remembering what she went through with the last nigga, Jonas released Sunshine, then started pacing the floor. "I told you this nigga wasn't gonna stop until you dealt with that money situation.

"I don't wanna talk about that shit!" she yelled, pissing him off even more.

"I told your ass this shit wasn't over as long as you had his money! What if we were home with Mya? What if I was at work and you were here by yourself with Mya? Shit fucked up and you don't wanna talk about it?"

Sunshine stomped up the steps. "Fuck this shit, I'm going to bed."

Jonas yelled, "You need to grow the fuck up, Sunshine!"

Taking a seat on the couch, Jonas realized his cousin might have been right when she told him that sometimes love couldn't overpower someone loving toxic behavior. Sunshine was so accustomed to dealing with toxic people that she didn't know how to live without it, even if that meant creating her own problems.

Entering the bedroom, Sunshine couldn't believe how fucked up it was. She then walked to Mya's room. Seeing the baby room was still how they left it, she knew Monsta was behind it all. Seeing as it'd been months since she heard from him, she couldn't help but to wonder what made him start fucking with her again after all the time that passed. When Sunshine turned around to leave Mya's room, she was frightened by Jonas standing there.

"Damn, you scared me, Jonas."

Jonas pulled her into a hug. "My bad, baby. Look, I don't want to fight or anything about this shit. I was thinking that maybe I could book you a nice room, Jacuzzi and all for a week or so, and I'll start on the house as soon as the sun comes up. What do you think about that?"

Sunshine smiled. That right there is the very reason she loved him. She just stormed away from him after giving him attitude and here he was trying to make things right between them. He spoiled her and that's all she ever wanted.

"What about Mya?"

"I'll pay your mom and sister to keep her longer, or I'll see if one of my cousins can get her for us. Stop trying to find a way to go against what I need you to do."

"I'm not, baby."

"Go pack your bag and I'll call around to see who has anything available because it is late."

Jonas went back downstairs to find his wife somewhere to stay while she got her things together. Sunshine had a few outfits in her suitcase already downstairs, but since she really didn't plan on doing too much of nothing, she wanted to grab some regular clothes. Besides, when she was out of town, she was half naked most of the time.

"What the fuck?" Sunshine said as she opened up her underwear drawer.

There was an envelope addressed to her. She knew by the handwriting that it was in fact from Monsta. As bad as she wanted to open it and read it, she decided to wait until Jonas took her to the room. The last thing she wanted to do is have Jonas walk in while she was reading the letter.

Being anxious, Sunshine quickly grabbed some stuff then rushed downstairs. "Jonas, I'm ready."

"So, I found a spot downtown and booked the room for a week. I'm gonna call Poppa in the morning and see if he has time to help me get this shit together."

"Alright. Come on, let's get out of here," she ordered.

Jonas made it downtown in no time. Sunshine was so tired and ready to go to bed that she damn near begged him to hurry up and get there. They checked in and Jonas carried her bags to her room.

"I'm about to go back to the house and crash, but if you need anything, don't hesitate to hit me up."

Sunshine showered her husband with kisses. "I love you so much, baby. Go home and get some rest, my love."

"I love you too. I want you to get some rest too, and I'll handle everything like the house and Mya in the morning."

They shared another kiss before Jonas left to go home. He was going ask his family for help, but he had a feeling that it wouldn't be as easy as the first time they helped.

After a hot shower, Sunshine threw on a t-shirt before grabbing the letter out of her bag. She was ready to read Monsta's letter and count how many times he called her a bitch. To her surprise, he wasn't as wild as usual.

Sunshine,

Look, I really do love and miss your ass so much. I'm fucked up in here not being able to hold or make love to you anymore. On top of that, I wanna meet my daughter. I don't care about the bullshit you did with that other nigga, y'all my family and can't anything change that. Do me a favor and go check on my mom. I fucked up with her again and haven't been able to talk to her in a while. I've changed for the better, and I want us to become a family again. From now on, I don't wanna be beefed out with you. I want nothing but love. Never forget that I was the nigga who kept that pussy soaked even when you made me mad.

Love always and forever

Monsta

P.S. I just got a new phone. Call me. 313-524-5555

Looking down at the rock that Jonas placed on her hand, she shook her head as she folded the letter back up. He was trying to be the nice Monsta, but she couldn't fall for that shit. As she laid down, she tried not to think about the letter, but when he said he kept her pussy wet, she couldn't help but to think he was also the same nigga who kept her eyes soaked with tears.

"I hate you so much," she mumbled before closing her eyes.

Keisha laid across the bed not knowing what her next move was. Whatever little money she did have was spent on her room and food, but things were getting tight for her. If she wasn't so scared the detectives would find her, she would've went to the hood to find one of her old tricks and made some money. One thing's for sure, her pussy got wetter when her pockets got dry, and she knew how to make a few bucks with Lil' Mama.

"Damn, let me get up and make some moves," she mumbled to herself. It was 12pm and if she didn't make shit pop off, it would be her last day there.

After getting dressed, Keisha was ready to hit the streets. Being downtown, she paid more for a room, but there were a lot of businessmen with money, which meant her type of men. Keisha stepped on the elevator wearing her big shades, hoping to not be spotted by the wrong people.

"Keisha?" Sunshine questioned.

Raising her head, Keisha saw Sunshine standing there. She always thought if they ever were to bump into each other it was gonna be a fight. But seeing Sunshine just staring at her and not knocking her head off, she wasn't sure what was going to happen.

"Hey," Keisha said, trying to rush off the elevator as soon as the door opened.

Sunshine wasn't even on a fighting tip, especially after getting her ass beat by Kyrah not too long ago. She really just wanted to see how she'd been doing after all this time.

"Keisha, wait!" she said, grabbing the back of Keisha's dress.

"Look, Sunshine, I don't want to fight. I'm sorry for everything, and I'm paying for it now. Yeah, that's right. Karma is fucking me up as we speak," Keisha said, damn near in tears.

Sunshine could tell her ex best friend was going through a lot by her appearance. Although she was pregnant, she hadn't gained any weight for real, and she was so stressed out that her edges were gone. Those sneaky links with Monsta weren't even worth it in the end.

"Hey, I'm about to go get some breakfast, join me."

Keisha gave her a strange look.

"My treat," Sunshine said, closing the deal.

Keisha smiled. "Alright, sounds like a plan."

As the two ex-best friends sat across from each other, Sunshine couldn't help but to wonder what Keisha had been up to. The last time she heard anything about her was when Monsta beat her ass real bad, and she called the police on him. It's crazy how she never had the balls to do that herself.

"You really wanted to be Monsta's baby mama so bad that you would say fuck me and my feelings just to fuck him?"

Keisha knew this conversation had to happen one day, and she was all for it. She shocked Sunshine with her story. "First of all, let me tell you that I was fucking Monsta years before you were even in the picture. When he hooked up with you, I damn near begged you not to fall for his shit, but you didn't listen to me."

"What? Bitch, are you serious?!" Sunshine yelled, damn near choking on her food.

"Yeah, dead ass. It wasn't no love type shit like what y'all had. I was more of the bitch that fucked the crew when they needed to bust a quick nut and didn't feel like going home to their main bitch."

Sunshine shook her head. She knew her friend was a hoe but damn. It was crazy how Monsta had been telling her about Keisha for the longest, but she never wanted to believe the stories. Hearing all of this coming out her mouth was a different type of hurt.

"You saying y'all were just fucking, right? When did you decide to carry his child? I mean, he was so happy about me being pregnant, I would have never guessed he would get someone else pregnant too."

"I gotta be completely honest with yo, because we were once best friends. Monsta wanted to call shit off for good with me. At first, I was cool with that, but over time, I realized I didn't wanna keep fucking his friends. I wanted him for myself."

Sunshine put her head down. She thought she could handle the truth about everything, but hearing the betrayal was slowly killing her inside.

"We were best friends. I told you everything about us, from the abuse to him getting caught up with other bitches. I even told you about him forcing himself on me whenever I was mad and didn't want to fuck him. What in your mind made you think he would be perfect for you? What would make you cross me for him?"

At the time everything went down, Keisha allowed jealousy to take over and actually thought she was getting one up on Sunshine by still fucking with Monsta. Soon, no longer giving a fuck about their friendship, Keisha put her plan into motion. Now she wanted to cry for hurting her friend, but the damage was already done.

"I'm so sorry for everything I've done to hurt you, Sunshine. I know I was wrong and I just want you to know that the bitch Karma is kicking my ass right now."

"As she should," Sunshine simply said, sipping on her orange juice.

Keisha wanted to tell her the whole truth about how she was so desperate for Monsta to be hers that she stole his sperm. After giving it some thought, she didn't want to fuck up any chance of them becoming friends again.

"So, I heard about Monsta and what he did to you and the baby. I'm sorry you had to go through that."

Keisha knew she was on that bullshit with him, but she didn't think she deserved to be damn near beat to death with her unborn child. "Thanks. You know the police were called on him and now everything is so fucked up for me."

Sunshine could tell by the tears forming in her eyes and the way her body shook that she had a painful story to tell, but she was all ears. "What's going on, Keisha?"

Keisha hesitated to respond at first, not sure if she could tell Sunshine what was going on. Then she thought about how she was the one that betrayed their friendship, not her.

"After checking out of the hospital, some detectives came to talk to me. They want me to snitch on everyone."

Keisha started to cry, and Sunshine couldn't help but to hug her ex best friend. "It's gonna be alright, Keisha."

"It's not, and I'm scared shitless."

"What are you gonna do, girl?" Sunshine questioned.

Keisha wiped her eyes. "Girl, they talking about locking me up if I don't bring them whatever it is they're asking for. I don't wanna help them with this shit. I just wanna move on with my life."

"They can't lock you up. We both know you ain't have shit to do with Monsta's bullshit."

Tears still rolled down Keisha's face. "I moved out of my apartment just so they wouldn't be able to find me. To be honest, after today, I don't know what my next move is. I'm fucked either way. If I tell on him then I'm dead, and if he gets out, I'm dead. I grew up too fast, not really doing shit with my life, and now I finally realize I wanna live a long life with my baby and probably won't have a chance now."

"Damn, Keisha, I'm so sorry you got caught up in this bullshit. Shit got rocky between us, but I wanna help you and the baby. We were once good friends. I can't just walk away from you."

Keisha could tell from her tone that she was genuine and still cared about her. She wasn't sure how she could help her out, but she was grateful.

"I'm gonna go pay for breakfast then we can go back to the room. I have an idea how I can help you."

Once back at the room, Sunshine set up an Uber so she could go back to her house.

"What the hell are you doing here, Sunshine?" Jonas asked, still cleaning up.

"I forgot something," she simply responded as she ran up the stairs to her bedroom.

Poppa watched Sunshine go upstairs. He liked her for the most part and thought that she was good for his brother, but he could tell she was up to something.

"What's that all about, bro?"

Jonas played it off. "Shit, I don't know. That girl's attitude be having me confused as hell sometimes."

They both laughed.

"That's probably why I haven't found the right one to settle down with. I can't deal with all that bipolar shit."

Jonas laughed. "She's not bipolar, she's just learning how to love again," Jonas tried to explain.

Poppa took a seat on the couch. He had helped out downstairs all morning and was dead tired.

"I'll order some food or something, bro. I really appreciate your help."

Poppa shook his head in agreement. Eating some good, unhealthy food sounded good at the moment.

Sunshine returned downstairs with a bag. "What's that, baby?"

Sunshine rushed over to place a kiss on his lips.

"The end of all my problems."

Not really understanding what she was talking about, Jonas shook his head in agreement.

"Alright, if you say so."

Sunshine then turned her attention to Poppa.

"Thanks once again for saving my home, I really appreciate it."

"No problem, sis. You know I got y'all back. Oh yeah, congratulations on the wedding. I would have brought a gift, but I didn't find out until I got here."

Sunshine giggled. "It's alright. We planned on celebrating with everyone but came home to this bullshit."

"Alright, I understand that. By the way shit going, we'll be partying in no time."

"Hell yeah," Jonas added in.

Sunshine gave Jonas another kiss. "I'll call you later, baby."

Trying to help her friend, Sunshine rushed back to Keisha, but this time, in her own car. Her plan was to give Keisha the bag full of Monsta's money so she could skip town and get the fuck away from Detroit and those crooked cops that were trying to pin her for Monsta's bullshit.

Sunshine knocked on Keisha's door. "Keisha, it's Sunshine."

Keisha looked through the peephole to confirm it was her friend and just her alone. She could never be too careful.

"Dang, girl, that was quick. Now, how are you gonna help solve my problem?"

Sunshine handed over the bag. It was way less than what she took, but anything could help Keisha out in her situation. Keisha's mouth dropped open when she saw the money in the bag. She never expected Sunshine to come through the way she did.

"Oh my God! Are you serious? This is for me?"

Keisha pulled Sunshine into a tight hug to show her appreciation. "Thank you so much, Sunshine. You just don't know how much this really means to me. I love you, girl!" she cried.

"It's all good, Keisha. I just want you to get the fuck on and never look back. Go to a whole new state and take care of that baby. Staying here will only get you hurt."

Tears rolled down their faces as they hugged. They were grown enough to realize Monsta played them both. They needed to have each other's back, especially when it came to him.

Later that night while Keisha was in her room planning her escape from Detroit, Sunshine sat in her room thinking about all the bullshit Keisha shared about

Monsta. Although she let Keisha's fucked up story get the best of her and couldn't beat her ass like she always thought she would, she wanted to go off on Monsta's ass. Then she thought about how she did have a way to contact his ass. As she read over his letter and saw how he had tried to be nice, the more she hated him. Once again, he tried to play on her feelings. Not only did she hate him for her, but Keisha too. Sunshine slowly dialed his number on the room phone.

"Who dis'?" Monsta calmly said into the phone, sending chills through Sunshine's body.

She hated him, but his voice still did something to her.

"Why did you want me to call you?" she questioned, getting straight to the point.

Monsta smiled. "You sound sexy as hell. I miss you, love."

"I'm not trying to hear that shit, boy."

Monsta laughed at her. "Yeah right, muthafucka, you wouldn't have called if you didn't. Facetime me so I can see you, baby."

Sunshine shook her head, knowing he was trying to play on her. "Nah, you good."

Monsta knew Sunshine always loved his voice and was easily turned on by it. "Why you playin' with me, baby? I know for a fact those panties wet as fuck by now."

Sunshine knew she had to take control of the situation, or he'd have her ass completely turned on and playing with her pussy over the phone.

"Stop talking to me like that or I'm gonna hang up," she demanded.

Monsta kept laughing at her. "Yo' nigga must be around 'cause you actin' funny as fuck."

"I don't have a nigga. I have a real boss that loved me enough to put a ring on my hand."

"What?"

Sunshine loved that she could now hurt him and get him in his feelings. "Yeah, that's right. I'm married now."

Monsta's smile was long gone. "Fuck that bitch ass nigga! Do that nigga know you a fuckin' ran thru, bipolar ass bitch?"

Now Sunshine was laughing at him. "Bipolar? Really? Bipolar? Monsta, that's all you. And I have never been run thru, bitch."

Monsta held the phone thinking of how he should handle this. He wanted to go the fuck off, but at the same time, he didn't want her to hang up and never call him again.

"I heard that nigga of yours playing house with you and my baby."

"And? He's doing a great job at it too!" she snapped.

Monsta wished she was in front of him so he could choke the life out of her. He also knew it was one of two reasons she was popping off at the mouth like that. One, Jonas was right there listening. Or two, because she knew he couldn't lay hands on her at the moment.

"Bitch, he can have you, but I'm coming back to get my baby," Monsta calmly said.

"Your name isn't on a fucking birth certificate or anything. Mya knows who her daddy is." Sunshine finally knew what could hurt Monsta and played on his emotions.

"Mya loves her daddy so much, I don't think she'll ever love anyone as much as him. Even in my stomach, she kicked and played with him every time he touched or talked to my belly. She never did that with you because she knew you wouldn't be a good daddy to her."

"You a stupid bitch actin' like I can't get you touched from in here. I'll kill you and that nigga. I don't mind leaving her an orphan. Shid, I'll leave Mya an orphan before I let y'all be happy with her."

"Touched like how you had somebody fuck my house up and leave that note. You right, your goons really trashed my house. Stop making these fake threats and worry about not dropping the soap and becoming somebody's bitch," Sunshine sarcastically said.

"Fuck you, bitch. I swear when I get out, I'ma make you my bitch again."

"You know what? I wish Keisha would go ahead and give those detectives the info on you so you can spend the rest of your fuckin' life locked up. Crazy bitch ass nigga," Sunshine said, laughing.

"Alright, bitch, you think shit funny. Jonas Antwon Bentley. 19728 W. 7 Mile. Boom. Boom." With that being said, Monsta hung up.

As Sunshine tore the letter up and flushed it down the toilet, she realized the address he recited was Jonas' shop, *Bentley Cuts*. Panicking, she quickly tried to call Monsta back, but he didn't answer. Being desperate, Sunshine tried calling a few more times and even left messages begging him not do anything crazy. Since he wouldn't pick up or respond, she felt like it was too late.

Sunshine packed her bags so she could go home. At that point, she didn't care if the house was fucked up or not. She wanted and needed to be under Jonas. Going back to Keisha's room, Sunshine told her she was leaving and that since her room was paid for, she could just stay there until she left Detroit. Keisha was all for it and happy that she hadn't paid for her room yet. Sunshine rushed home to be with her husband, wishing she would've just left shit alone.

Walking into the house, she saw Jonas knocked out on the couch. Knowing she had once again fucked up, tears rolled down her cheeks. The thought of something bad happening to him because of her scared her. She even thought about leaving him just to keep him safe but knew he loved her and Mya enough to go looking for her, not caring about the consequences. After dropping her bags Sunshine climbed on the couch, laying on his chest.

"What are you doing back here? I told you I just needed another day or so," he said, still half asleep.

He waited a minute to hear her respond, but when she didn't, he looked down to see her crying. "What's wrong, baby?"

"I just love you so much, Jonas."

"I love you too, but you ain't got to cry about it." Jonas gave his wife a kiss. "You know you can talk to me if you need to get something off your chest."

"I'm good, Jonas. Can you just hold me so I can get some rest?"

Jonas hugged her a little tighter like she asked. He knew when something was bothering her and hated how she never felt comfortable talking about it. He hoped that in due time, she would get out of that.

The next morning, Jonas snuck off the couch so he could shower. He had been on some bullshit and needed to get to the shop. Although Meka had been holding shit down and getting paid to cover his ass, he needed to get back to being the boss.

Jonas placed a kiss on Sunshine's lips just before he tried to walk out of the door.

"Where are you going?" Sunshine asked as she jumped up.

"Work. I've missed more than a few days and need to go in."

Sunshine wasn't trying to hear that. She jumped off the couch, fearing the worst. "You can't go in today, Jonas." She started to cry.

"What the hell is wrong with you, Sunshine? You've been on some crybaby shit since you got back yesterday. What the fuck happened at the room?"

"Nothing, I just…"

"You just what Sunshine?"

Sunshine stood there crying. How was she going tell him she called Monsta talking shit and now he had her scared?

Jonas didn't like the way she was acting and her not saying shit worried him. "Talk to me baby, please."

"Just don't leave me."

Jonas had plans on going back to work, but the way Sunshine held on to him and begged him to stay, he knew he couldn't leave her like that.

Keisha spent the whole morning going over her plans. Thanks to Sunshine, she had enough funds to finally make it out of Detroit and far away from Monsta and his bullshit. She knew without her, he'd be able to walk free in no time.

Standing in the shower, Keisha thought she heard a strange noise. Not knowing for sure, she stood there for a second trying to see if she would hear it again. After a short pause and not hearing anything, she finished letting the water rinse the soap off her body. She turned the water off then pulled the shower curtain open.

"Aye, bitch, Monsta said what up."

The masked man in all black let off two shots before she could even let out a scream. Before leaving, he grabbed the bag of money on the table in the front room. Monsta didn't mention any money, so he wasn't either. Keisha and her unborn baby never had a chance after being shot once in the head and once in the chest.

"No, Jonas."

Jonas slid out the bed. It was 6am and he wanted to get to the shop before Meka.

"Come on, baby, don't do this shit every fucking morning. I've been home with you for two days now, I gotta go to the shop," he tried to explain then took a seat next to Sunshine on the bed. "What's up, baby? What the hell is going on that got you like this? Why are you acting like you don't want me to leave the house?"

"I just want you to stay here with me."

Jonas still felt like it was more to the story, and she was on some bullshit. "How about you get dressed and come to the shop with me today? I missed too many days. I'm sure you can help with some paperwork or something."

Sunshine thought about what he was saying before agreeing to spend the day with him. Even though she didn't really want to leave the house, she didn't want to be by herself.

Just as he wanted, Jonas beat Meka to the shop and was ready to work. He knew a few people were waiting for him to show his face again, and he didn't want to let anyone down.

"Look what the cat done dragged in. Congratulations on the wedding that I wasn't invited to," Meka said as she gave Sunshine and Jonas a hug.

"Yeah, I had to come back. I think people forgot who the real boss is."

Meka laughed. "Oh, don't get cocky like I wasn't holding it down for a little over a month."

Hearing Meka say a little over a month caught Sunshine's attention. She thought he'd only missed that week they were out of town and the last few days. Jonas stared at the floor, trying not to look Sunshine's way. A part of him wished he would have been man enough to come clean but getting married sounded better at the time. "Let's go make sure everything is set up," he said to Meka just to get her out of the office. He then turned to Sunshine. "You gon' be alright in here?"

"Yeah, baby. I'm actually about to call my mom and check on Mya."

After placing a kiss on her lips, Jonas stepped out, making sure to shut the door behind him.

"Meka, she doesn't know about my problem. Try not to bring that up in front of her."

Meka shook her head. "You snuck off and got married. Don't you think your wife should know about your problem?"

"I dealt with it. It's not a problem of mine anymore."

"Yeah, alright, Jonas. What if it happens again?" she questioned.

Jonas took a seat in his work area. "I got her, it ain't coming back."

Meka decided to drop the subject. Jonas is the type of guy that once he made his mind up, that was it.

Jonas greeted Poppa. "What's up, bro bro?"

"What's up, bro. Glad to see you back in this bitch. Can you line me up right quick before everyone gets here?"

"Sit your ass down, I got you."

In no time, Jonas was done and people had started to walk in. Most heard Jonas was coming back and were ready for him to bless them with a cut. Sunshine sat at the desk answering the phone and making appointments. That's when something hit her. After her high school graduation, she went to school to do hair, but she never did anything with her license. Her mom talked major shit to her about not doing anything but following Monsta around in the past, but now this could be her chance to do something with her life.

Just thinking about life, she thought about Keisha and everything she was going through. She decided to give her a call and see if she was able to leave safely. After not getting an answer, she decided to call again. Once again, still no answer. Sunshine didn't like that and got a strange feeling in the pit of her stomach. She decided to call the front desk. After talking to the lady at the front desk, she was told she hadn't checked out yet. Sunshine requested someone go to her room and check on Keisha. She had to ask using her own name seeing as she gave Keisha her room. Sunshine felt sick to her stomach every second she waited for the hotel to call her back with any details about Keisha.

Chapter 6

"Aye, man, I've been trying to reach you for the last few days. Everything was handled."

Monsta sat up in his bunk. "Alright, good looking. After everything is confirmed, I'll hit that account up."

Darryl hung the phone up, worried. He wanted Monsta to just send him the money, so he could get the fuck on. What he didn't tell Monsta is that he didn't realize it was Keisha and not Sunshine in the room that morning until the shots were fired. So, not only did he kill the wrong person, but he was gon' try to play it off hoping Monsta would send him the money without checking shit out.

That night, while they all sat in the rec room watching TV, the 6:00pm news came on. Monsta smiled at the breaking news. Just hearing about a young lady getting murdered at the motel did something to his soul. Then it hit him that a muthafucka really killed his baby mama. He started to feel bad and realized he wanted Darryl killed now.

He continued to listen to the news reporter, but shit wasn't adding up. The reporter mentioned the victim being pregnant, and he knew for sure that was wrong. He knew Sunshine wasn't carrying that nigga's baby already. That's when Keisha's picture popped up on the screen. A part of him was happy that Darryl fucked up, but he still needed to die.

Returning to his cell, Monsta laid back plotting on how he was gonna get that nigga back.

"What's on your mind, Cuz?"

"Shit, just trying to make it home to my baby," Monsta calmly said.

After some time, he learned not to do too much talking around that nigga Rock because he ran his mouth, and he didn't like that. Monsta was really waiting for the right moment to take him out.

As Rock went to sleep, Monsta couldn't wait to talk to Darryl.

Sunshine screamed then burst into tears. She was laying in the bed watching the news when she got the terrible news that Keisha was murdered.

Jonas ran up the stairs. "What's wrong, baby?"

Sunshine couldn't even answer him. All she could do is point at the TV and cry. Jonas held her in his arms as he listened to the report of Keisha and her unborn child's murder.

"Damn, baby, I'm so sorry about your friend."

Sunshine continued to cry hard. "It's all my fault. It's all my fault, Jonas."

"Stop blaming yourself for this shit. It's not your fault, baby," he said, rubbing her back, trying to calm her down.

"She would still be alive if it wasn't for me."

Jonas knew she'd been different since coming home from the motel early, and he prayed he could finally get some answers.

"Baby, come sit and talk to me. I need to know everything, so that I can protect you. Trust me, baby, I got your back no matter what."

It took Sunshine a while to calm down, even after Jonas brought her up a nice cup of hot tea.

"Jonas, I swear I thought I was doing the right thing and only fucked up even more."

"Tell me what happened, baby. I need to know everything."

Sunshine sipped on her tea. "I did something I shouldn't have and now my friend is dead when it should've been me."

"Does this have anything to do with Monsta?" he questioned.

Sunshine knew it was time to tell him the truth about everything. "Baby, it has everything to do with him."

Not coming completely out with the story, Jonas felt like she was about to be on some bullshit. "What the fuck is going on?"

"Monsta had someone trash the house, and I found a letter from him. He left his number and asked me to call, but I didn't the first night I was there."

"So, you did call that nigga?" Jonas asked, jumping up from the bed.

Feeling like he was about to flip out, Sunshine tried to calm him down. "Jonas, please! I swear it wasn't like that!" she yelled, following him out the room.

"Then how the fuck was it, Sunshine? Every time I bring that nigga's name up, you catch an attitude. Now you hittin' this nigga up while he locked up. Do you still want that nigga?"

"Baby, my best friend was just killed and you worried about that?"

Jonas was furious. "You know what? I really do see why that nigga was going upside your fuckin' head. You say and do fucked up shit like you live and love this toxic shit."

Sunshine was pissed. "All this time I thought I was with a real boss and married a good guy, and now I find out the truth. You sound real happy that a nigga used to abuse me. You know what? Fuck you, Jonas! Get the fuck out my house!"

"Fuck me?"

Sunshine jumped in his face. "Yeah, fuck you, nigga!"

Jonas snatched Sunshine up by her shirt. "You too fucking stupid to realize when a muthafucka really love your crazy ass."

For a moment, Sunshine thought he was going to hit her and they would be in that bitch fighting, but he was a real man. Seeing she was uncomfortable, Jonas let her shirt go.

"I'm sorry for that, but you do some fucked up shit."

"I fucked up, Jonas, and I'm sorry. What more do you want me to say?"

Jonas had so much love for Sunshine, but it couldn't stop him from wanting to walk away from her. She admitted to calling the one who broke her down, and that shit hurt him. Once again feeling like Monsta still had some type of control over his wife, Jonas started walking down the stairs.

"Where are you going, Jonas?"

"I think it'll be best to give you some space so you can decide if this is really what you want. I love you, but if you still want him, you need to just say that."

"I don't want him. I want the man that I married," she cried.

Jonas stopped at the front door with her right behind him. "Why the fuck did you call him? What did y'all need to talk about?"

Sunshine was crying, but that wasn't making Jonas ease up.

"You called that nigga 'cause you wanted something. What the fuck is it? What I'm not doing to make you happy?" he yelled, making her cry harder.

"You're doing everything right, Jonas. I told you he sent that note I just called to tell him I was happily married and all that talking about us getting back together and him seeing Mya was over. I called thinking I was ending shit for good but ended up getting my friend and her unborn baby killed."

Jonas could tell it tore her up and didn't hesitate to pull her into a hug. "You can't keep blaming yourself for the fucked-up shit he does."

"This time, I have to take blame."

Jonas led her over to the couch and listened to her tell him about Keisha dealing with the crooked detective and giving her the money to leave town.

"Baby, you meant well by trying to help her," he said, trying to calm her down.

"I called Monsta from the motel phone so he couldn't call me back. I wasn't thinking when I let Keisha have the room for the rest of the week after talking shit to him. I didn't think he would send someone after me. He wanted me dead for real this time."

Jonas knew, when it came down to it, Monsta had to die. He wasn't into all that street shit anymore but when it came to his family, he'd do whatever to keep them safe.

"I got you, baby. You know I'm not gonna let anything happen to you or Mya. Do you trust me to keep my word?"

"Yes, Jonas I do. Can you forgive me for creating this mess?"

Jonas planted a kiss on her lips. "Yes, baby. I just need you to talk to me before you make any decisions from now on."

Jonas held Sunshine in his arms until she was asleep.

Although he was trying to be a business owner and family man, Monsta was getting ready to have to deal with the Bentley Boys.

Darryl sat outside of the house so no one could hear his phone conversation with Monsta. It'd been two weeks since he did a job for Monsta, and he still hadn't gotten paid yet. He figured Monsta must've gotten in trouble and that's why he hadn't heard from him. He was surprised he finally got that call.

"What's up, Monsta? I was reaching out for my bread."

Monsta laughed. "You really are trying to play in my face? Bitch, I saw the news."

Darryl shook his head knowing he fucked up. Now he felt like he should've just taken the bag of money he got from the motel and got the fuck on. Trying to be greedy wasn't getting him anywhere.

"Shit moved so fast. I didn't realize who that bitch was until I shot her," Darryl stuttered to get out.

Monsta knew he was speaking straight bullshit but decided he needed to use him for one more thing.

"I got another job for you," Monsta whispered as he checked to make sure Rock was still asleep.

Darryl knew this shit with Monsta was gonna be a long-term thing, he just wished he could see some money now. "I'm gonna need some funds in my account, Monsta."

"Your funky ass ain't did shit I asked you to do yet. Bitch, you owe me."

Darryl shook his head. "Look, I got something for you now that's worth some bread. If I send it to you, you gotta cash me out."

"What the fuck you got, nigga?" Monsta asked.

Darryl quickly sent over a picture that he was able to sneak of Mya, right along with Sunshine's phone number.

"What the fuck is this?" Monsta mumbled as he checked his messages.

Darryl waited to be blessed. "How much for that?"

Monsta didn't answer. It was his first time seeing his daughter and that had his full, undivided attention at the time.

"Aye, man, you gon' cash me out or what?"

"I'll call your bitch ass back." Monsta hung up the phone.

Looking at his baby girl caused his brain not to think of all the evil thoughts in his head. He couldn't help but to smile hard at the beautiful baby girl he helped bring into this world. She for sure had his eyes, but she was as beautiful as her mother.

"My baby girl Mya. You so fuckin' beautiful, daddy can't wait to see you in person. I promise, baby girl, daddy will be out soon, and you best believe I'm coming to get you."

Monsta was so busy looking at Mya, he didn't even notice that Darryl gave him Sunshine's number at first. It wasn't until later that night after count when he pulled his phone back out that he saw her number.

"Hello," Sunshine said into the phone, still half asleep.

"You know if he would have killed you, I was gon' kill him. To be honest, I'm still gonna kill him." Monsta explained.

Hearing his voice talking about killing someone woke Sunshine all the way up. "How the fuck you get my number?"

Jonas jumped up, snatching the phone from his wife. "You know whenever I see you, I'm gon' beat yo' bitch ass, right?"

Monsta laughed. "You know how many niggas say that shit and when they see me, they be on their best behavior? Look, bitch, you nor any other nigga put fear in my heart."

"Stay the fuck away from my family, dog."

It pissed Jonas off that every time he said something, Monsta would laugh like a fucking dumb ass.

"I busted in that bitch and made that baby, nigga. That's my fucking family," Monsta said, still laughing.

Before hanging up, Jonas yelled in the phone

"Fuck you bitch!"

Jonas turned his attention to Sunshine.

"How the fuck that nigga get your number? Didn't you tell me you called him from the motel phone?"

"I swear I did, baby. I don't know how he got my number this time or any other time," Sunshine tried to explain.

"I'm not going to the shop today. I think we need to go get Mya."

"I agree. I miss my baby anyways. With all this shit going on, she didn't need to be out of our sight."

Sunshine climbed out the bed, but noticed Jonas didn't get up with her. "What's wrong, baby?"

"I'm tired of this nigga and this crazy bullshit."

Sunshine felt bad because she knew everything was her fault and she brought all this drama into Jonas' life.

"I'm so sorry, Jonas. Please don't hate me," Sunshine begged.

Jonas stood up so he could hug her and show her some love. There was so much shit going on, but he wanted her to know that no matter what, he had her back. At this point, if he had to kill to bring peace in their life, that's just what he had to do.

Before Jonas joined Sunshine in the shower, he called Meka to let her know about everything going on. She'd never really heard the old Jonas speak up in a while and by that, she knew he wasn't playing behind his wife and child. At the shop, Meka let the family know Jonas was going through some shit and later at cousin night, they all needed to talk and get on board with going to war.

Jonas and Sunshine both played in Mya's face, praying for nothing but her safety.

"Ma, can I ask you a question?"

"What, child?" Ms. Mathews asked, still watching TV.

Sunshine didn't know how to ask, so she got straight to the point. "Did you give anyone my number?"

"Now why would you ask me something so stupid like that? If I'm not at work, I'm here all damn day. Who would I possibly give your number to?"

"My bad, Ma. I know it wasn't you. This whole Monsta bullshit got me scared, and I don't know who's behind all this shit."

Ms. Mathews shook her head. "I tried to tell you about that nigga. I knew from jump he wasn't shit."

Sunshine rolled her eyes. "Yeah, Ma, I know. I've heard this story over a thousand times before."

"And you best believe every time I hear that muthafucka's name I'ma bring that shit up."

Jonas didn't pay them any mind. He was just happy to have Mya smiling in his face. That nigga Monsta sat up on the phone talking about how this is his family and Mya is his, but the way her face lit up seeing Jonas, there wasn't shit anybody could say. Mya is his baby and that's all there was to it.

"Where is Zoey?"

"She's in her room. Nasty ass been up all night busting it open for Darryl's junky ass."

"What? I hope my baby wasn't around that shit."

"Hell nah. I don't trust that nigga for real. He be lookin' all crazy like he high or something. That nigga up to no good."

That caught Jonas' attention. "What do you mean by that? What the hell is he up to?"

Ms. Mathews laughed, trying to play it off. "I'm just talking."

Sunshine and Jonas gave her a strange look.

"Ma, that ain't shit to play about, but let me go talk to your daughter."

Jonas didn't care what she said, he knew she said that shit for a reason. He made a mental note to watch his ass from now on.

Sunshine opened her sister's bedroom door.

"Wake up, Zoey."

Zoey didn't move. Sunshine didn't call out for her again. Instead, she took this moment to look around her room. First stop was her drawers.

"Ok, bitch, you better not be hiding shit," she mumbled.

Not finding shit, she searched through the closet. Sunshine then noticed something that looked real familiar. "Oh, hell nah!"

Picking up the empty bag that once held the money she gave to Keisha, Sunshine slapped Zoey in the face with it. "Bitch, what the fuck did you do?"

Zoey jumped up. "What the fuck you hit me for?"

Sunshine wasn't in the mood to talk. Instead, she swung on Zoey again. "You supposed to be my fucking sister."

Zoey wasn't sure why they were fighting, but she tried her best to fight back.

"I didn't do shit, stupid bitch!" she yelled.

Ms. Mathews jumped up to separate her daughters. She too had grown tired of their bullshit. Jonas sat Mya down in her car seat and was right behind his mother-in-law.

"I'll be back, Mya. Let me go get your crazy ass mama and auntie."

Jonas went straight to the room to break them up. Walking in, he could see that although their mother called herself breaking the fight up, she really was trying to hold Sunshine's hands, seeing as she was getting the best of the fight.

"Break this shit up!" Jonas yelled, stepping in between everyone.

Once they calmed down, he was able to pull Sunshine on one side of the bed while Ms. Mathews pulled Zoey to the other side.

"What the fuck is going on? I told y'all I'm sick and tired of all this fighting shit."

Zoey spoke out first. "I was asleep. This little stupid bitch came in here fighting me. I was just defending myself."

"What the fuck is going on, Sunshine?" Jonas asked.

At this point, Sunshine was crying. "Look, Jonas! Look at this bag."

Ms. Mathews was just as confused as Zoey. "What the fuck that bag got to do with you fighting your sister?"

Sunshine didn't trust the people that lived in that house any longer, so she gave Jonas all of her attention.

"Jonas, this is the bag that I had Monsta's money in. I gave this to Keisha," she cried out.

"Sunshine, that's not my bag!" Zoey yelled out, defending herself.

"Monsta sent somebody to kill me. Whoever it was took this bag and killed Keisha."

"Oh my God, Sunshine! You should know better than to think your sister would have anything to do with this shit," Ms. Mathews said.

There was a quick pause before everything started to make sense.

"Darryl! That was Darryl's bag!" Zoey screamed out.

Jonas was the first to run out of the room. He was ready to find and kill Darryl for every time he saw Sunshine scared or even crying. Everyone else was right behind him, on his ass.

"Where the fuck is Mya?"

Chapter 7

Monsta had been trying to keep a low profile and so far everything was going well. After learning the detectives had Keisha helping to bring him and his organization down, Monsta was happy Darryl did fuck up and kill her ass. He laughed knowing without Keisha and him being on his best behavior and staying out the hole, he'd be out in no time. With his fucked up way of thinking, he knew Sunshine still wanted him and wouldn't dare tell all the bullshit he'd been on lately.

"Damn. I got to cut all loose ends before a muthafucka has me jammed up," he mumbled just as Rock walked into the cell.

"What's up, Cuz?"

Monsta stared at him for a minute. He could tell he was up to no good. It was all in his face. Monsta never really fucked with niggas whose loyalty he had to question. Lately, he could tell Rock had either turned snake or had been one all along and he didn't know it.

"Fuck out my face, nigga."

Rock grimed him. "Fuck you too, nigga. I guess you hot shit 'cause they about to close your case. No face no case, right?"

Monsta stood up from his bunk. "Bitch, get out my business."

"Damn, now you know we better than that. Let's calm down and talk blood to blood. What you gon' do if they let you go? You thinking about gettin' your spot back on the streets or what?"

Monsta shook his head as he tried not to snap that nigga's neck right then and there. That bullshit conversation let him know the detective not only tried to get to Keisha, but his blood cousin as well.

"My spot? What you talkin' 'bout, Rock? When I get out, I'm going home to my baby and be the father she needs me to be. That's the spot I'm taking over. Matter of fact, I've been thinking about taking some cooking classes and maybe one day owning a food truck or something. Maybe when you get out, you can come work with me since we blood."

The look in Monsta's eyes and the tone of his voice told Rock his cover was blown. Rock damn near shitted on himself knowing he was next to die at the hands of Monsta. He shook his head, wanting to beg for forgiveness. Monsta wanted to kill him for turning snitch but knowing everyone was waiting to get him jammed up, he walked out of the cell with a smirk on his face. He had a few homies that wouldn't give a fuck about murking a muthafucka for him because they were already doing life.

Walking into one of his homies' cells, Monsta didn't say anything. He slipped him the cellphone he'd been using to handle his business.

"For sure, bro," Tony said as Monsta walked out. Tony wasted no time hiding the phone right along with his.

Monsta went back to his cell and waited for a guard to come get him for his appointment with his therapist. He had a story to tell. During their hour one session Monsta expressed how he felt like he was being followed around the jail. He made that move so if anything happened, he could have it in writing that they were out to get him all along.

"I've been working hard to get you out of this shit hole. To tell you the truth, everyone was against my decision at first, but I think I'm winning them over. They see that you're taking your medication, staying out the hole, and staying out of trouble. I have a little more fighting to do."

"A little more fighting to do? Fuck that mean?" She gave him a crazy look and Monsta corrected himself.

"I'm sorry. I meant to ask what that meant."

"That's better. Anyways, that means you might be going home soon."

Monsta smiled. "Are you serious?"

"Yes. I told you I was fighting for you. You might have to go home with meds, but you'll be at home with your daughter."

Monsta was escorted back to his cell with a big Kool-Aid smile on his face. It only left when he reached his cell and saw a few guards searching his room.

"What y'all doing? Y'all tearing my house up!" he yelled.

One guard stepped to his face. "Where's the phone, boy?"

"The phones are downstairs, but we can't use them until tomorrow afternoon."

"Stop playing with me, boy. We were told you had a phone and were using it to do dirt on the outside."

"Sorry, sir, but I don't know what you talkin' 'bout," Monsta said with an evil smirk on his face.

They tore his room up even more than what needed to be done, hoping to find something since Rock and Keisha fucked up. They were pissed no phone was found and their little inside man gave them nothing against him, which meant wasn't shit stopping him from leaving now. Knowing Rock been on some rat shit, Monsta was happy he was smart enough to hide the phone elsewhere. Monsta couldn't wait to laugh in Rock's face whenever he did come back into the room.

Monsta did make it his business to sneak back to Tony's room later that night to handle the last of his business before getting rid of the phone for good. Or so he thought. When he returned to his room before count, Monsta learned Rock was moved out of the cell they shared, and that was only more proof he was a snake. They must've known he would be killed for being a rat. Monsta was gonna get him killed but first, he wanted some time to pass just so he wouldn't be the first person they looked at. Tony was already on the job.

Turning his phone back on, Monsta watched as his screen reminded him he had ten messages and 20 missed calls. As he looked into it, he saw they were all from Darryl.

"I hope this muthafucka ain't calling about that bread he thinks I owe him," Monsta mumbled as he tried to call him back.

"What the fuck you callin' me for?"

"You played me on my money, so I decided to play you, nigga?"

Monsta laughed. "I don't talk crack language. Talk so I can understand yo' bitch ass."

"I'm glad you think everything fucking funny. I got a joke for you, nigga."

"What's that?" Monsta questioned.

"I got your daughter over here with me."

"Bitch, I'll kill you. Don't fuckin' play with your life like that," Monsta warned.

Darryl really didn't think things through. He was starting to believe he made a huge mistake by taking Mya.

"I just want my money, that's it. I'm not gonna hurt her," Darryl explained.

Monsta held the phone trying to think of how he could get his daughter and kill Darryl all while still locked up.

"Alright, take her to my mama's house. I need you to have my mama call me to verify my baby is with her and unharmed. Soon after, I'll make sure your account is nice and full."

Darryl liked that plan. "Alright, I can do that. I just want you to know this shit is all business."

"Oh yeah, nigga, I know how the game go."

Monsta wanted to get rid of the phone that night, but he needed to make sure his mama could reach him once Mya got there.

Sunshine sat on the couch crying her eyes out, rocking back and forth. Her baby was missing and nothing anyone said could make her calm down. Jonas was pissed off too, but instead of sitting there comforting her, he was pacing the floor and constantly repeating, "I can't believe this shit!"

"I'm so sorry, y'all, I had no clue what Darryl was up to."

Sunshine snapped. "Shut up, bitch! It ain't no telling. You probably were in on it with him."

Usually, Jonas would try to keep the peace between the sisters, but this time, he stayed out of it. He agreed with Sunshine. Maybe they did work together seeing how Zoey always acted like she was jealous of her sister.

Sunshine stood up. "I need to be out there looking for my baby."

"I called my cousins over. Wait for Meka to come get you."

"I don't want to wait on anybody, I wanna go now!" she yelled.

"Calm down, Sunshine, and call the police." Ms. Mathews ordered.

Neither Jonas nor Sunshine wanted to get the police involved. They felt like they would only accuse them of foul play and probably get locked up. Before Sunshine could say anything, Jonas' family was knocking on the door. Zoey let them all in. After speaking, Meka rushed over to Sunshine and pulled her into a hug.

"I'm so sorry, baby, but we got your back."

"Just get me out of this house and help me find my baby. I need my baby," she cried.

Sunshine followed Meka out the door, not saying shit to her mama or sister. Ain't no way they live in the same house as Darryl and didn't know shit about him working with Monsta all this time.

Once they gathered outside, Jonas held Sunshine as he told his cousins how Darryl was behind everything and had been working with Monsta all along.

"Let's go find this nigga then, cuz. You know we down for whatever," Mason said, lifting his shirt to show off his gun.

Everyone jumped in their cars ready to hit the streets to find baby Mya. Sunshine got in the car with Meka.

"Aye, Meka!" Jonas called out.

Meka jumped out of the car, wondering what he wanted.

"What's up cuz?"

Jonas and Meka had always been favorite cousins and counted on each other, so there was no surprise when Jonas damn near broke down to her.

"I need you to look out for my baby, man. She hurt not knowing where Mya at right now. Don't let her do anything stupid."

"Sunshine's my girl, I got you, cuz. You didn't even have to say shit."

Jonas hugged Meka. "I'll sit down for them and all y'all, you know that, right?"

"We'll do the same. Now go find Mya."

Everyone drove off in different directions searching for Darryl's car. They had promised to call one another if they saw him first. Jonas didn't want anyone to kill him because he needed to be the one to lay hands on his bitch ass.

Sunshine's legs shook as Meka drove around. She never imagined her baby would be kidnapped. Monsta did a lot of things, but kidnapping is a new low.

"This is all my fault. My baby is missing because I told Monsta Mya would never know him and she had a daddy."

"Stop that shit, Sunshine. This shit is not your fault, and that nigga gon' pay for this shit."

Sunshine cried harder. "I just want my baby back. She didn't do shit to nobody, she's just a baby."

"I know, girl. We're gonna find her," Meka assured her.

Mason cut the music down as he answered his phone for his sister.

"Where everyone at? I'm at Meka's house, ready for cousin night?"

"Damn, Nakia, we've been trying to reach your ass all night," Mason said into the phone.

Nakia smacked her lips. "I had a few shots and was knocked out. Anyways, why y'all not at Meka's house for cousin night?"

Mason shook his head. It hurt him to repeat the news to her, but he had to. "Somebody kidnapped Mya, and we all out here looking for her now."

"So, cousin night canceled?"

Mason wanted to hang up on his sister but tried to explain shit to her just in case she was still drunk. "I just told you somebody kidnapped Mya and we looking for her, what the fuck you think?"

"I was just asking. I don't see why y'all canceled our family night for somebody that's not family."

Mason shook his head at how ignorant his sister could be. He couldn't even respond to her stupid ass. Hanging up was the only way to handle that situation.

"What she talkin' about?" Poppa asked.

"A bunch of bullshit," he responded.

"I love my cousin, but she be on that bullshit."

Mason shook his head in agreement.

"Yeah, I know."

That night, everyone rode around searching high and low for Mya. At the end of the night, they all went home without her.

"Baby, go get in the bed and get you some rest."

"Jonas, we don't know where our baby is. I can't get no fuckin' rest until my baby comes home. Maybe we should get the police involved."

Jonas stopped pacing the floor long enough to wrap his arms around his wife. "I'm sorry, baby. I'm sorry I couldn't figure this shit out about Darryl earlier. I'm supposed to protect you and her from everything."

"Is my baby gon' come home and be alright?" she cried.

Jonas didn't want to make her any promises. At the same time, he couldn't disappoint her or hurt her any more than she had been. "We're gonna find her and kill everyone behind this shit."

"I love you, Jonas."

"Love you too, baby."

He saw she wasn't trying to lay down, so he went into the kitchen to make her a hot tea, which usually worked. He still wasn't sure about the police and tried his best to avoid the question.

Chapter 8

"Wake your lucky ass up!" the guard yelled, poking him with his baton.

Monsta slowly sat up. "Fuck you bothering me for?"

The guard smiled. "You lucky son of a bitch. How the fuck did you get so lucky?"

Monsta gave the guard, Timothy Brown, a strange look. "What the fuck your faggot ass talkin' about?"

"Word around here is you gettin' out later today?"

Monsta was still half asleep and not really in the mood for his bullshit. "Wake me up when it's time then, bitch."

Tim walked away. He could care less about the shit Monsta was talking. Monsta was known for running his mouth all the time because he was a little off. As soon as Tim was far away from his cell, Monsta got up to hang his sheet up. Most thought that meant he was taking a shit, but for real, he needed to handle his business.

He turned his phone back on. He saw he had one missed call. Calling the number back, he realized it was his mama's number when she spoke into the phone.

"What the fuck are you getting me mixed up in?!" Ms. Caldwell yelled into the phone.

"Hey, Ma," Monsta calmly said into the phone.

"Hi, Monsta, what's going on? This ugly, black ass nigga has been here since last night talking about him not leaving until we get in touch with you. Why is Mya here?"

"This shit really not my fault, Ma. Tell that nigga I'm about to send that cash now so he can get the fuck on."

"You on speaker phone so he hears you, she replied.

Darryl was scared but tried to act hard. In his head, he repeatedly prayed he made it out the house alive so he could get the fuck out of Detroit. The money he got from Keisha really wasn't enough for him to disappear all while having an addiction he couldn't kick, so he needed this bread. Monsta wasn't in the mood to even argue with him. As far as he was concerned, Darryl would be dead before the night was over with.

Darryl looked down at his account. "Hey, Monsta, like I said before, this shit was all business. Thanks for the nice payment."

"Bitch, get the fuck out my mama's house."

Darryl went ahead and left out, hoping he never had to see or hear from Monsta again.

"Tell me what the fuck is going on. I haven't heard from you in months, then this nigga drop this baby off because you owed him some money. I wanted to see my grandbaby but you didn't have to get somebody to kidnap her and bring her here."

"Ma, I didn't do this shit. Can you just make sure my baby good, and I'll handle everything else?"

"Yeah, you know I got you, Monsta," she said, not knowing just how much trouble he was putting her in.

Monsta texted one of his boys on the outside for a quick favor. He hated leaving loose ends around, and Darryl was a major problem.

Monsta: Need you, my boy.

Jerome: Got you. What's up.

Monsta: Darryl

Jerome: Say no more

After getting off the phone, Jerome got dressed knowing Darryl's dope fiend ass was probably at the spot somewhere trying to cop. He knew his job would be easy. Jerome ended up driving to three different spots Monsta ran looking for Darryl. He wasn't sure what he did and really didn't give two fucks. If Monsta needed him gone, that's what the fuck was gonna happen.

"Where the fuck this bitch ass nigga at?" he mumbled to himself as he turned the corner.

Darryl had just pulled up to the house after arguing with Zoey about some Sunshine bullshit. She also accused him of kidnapping Mya, which he denied. He thought that if he showed his face. Everyone would see she wasn't with him, and he wasn't responsible for her missing. After a good forty-five minutes, Zoey finally agreed to come out and talk to him.

"Make this shit quick," Zoey said with attitude.

Darryl tried to give her a hug, but she pushed him away.

"Damn, it's like that? Ok then," he said, acting like he really gave a fuck.

The other reason he was trying to act nice was to get in the house to get the money he stole from Keisha. The day before he came to the house, Mya was sitting in her chair in front of the TV when everyone was in Zoey's bedroom fighting and yelling. The idea of snatching Mya was only to make Monsta pay the money he owed him so he could get the fuck on.

"I see you still have a funky ass attitude."

"Where the fuck my niece at, muthafucka?" she snapped.

"I told you I don't have her. I hope y'all muthafuckas ain't go to the police with this bullshit. What the fuck I'ma do with a baby, and I don't even fuck with my own kids? And I'm not dropping any other babies off to my mama."

Zoey shook her head. "You a triflin ass nigga, and this is why I'm done with you."

Just as Darryl was about to go off and tell Zoey how he really felt, Ms. Mathews ran outside with a bat. Asking no questions, she swung, hitting Darryl in the shoulder with the bat.

"Where the fuck my granddaughter at, muthafucka?!"

Not giving him a chance to answer, Ms. Mathews kept swinging. Darryl tried to run to his car to avoid the hits, but that's when the gunshots rang out.

"Get down!" Ms. Mathews yelled.

Jerome lucked up pulling up to the house where he knew Darryl rested his head. When he pulled up, he was getting his ass beat with a bat by some older lady. Not giving a fuck, Jerome let them shots fire out before speeding off. Zoey sat up, looking around. Her first instinct told her to check on her mama.

"Ma, Ma you ok?" she yelled.

Slowly sitting up, she responded. "Yeah, I'm alright, just a little shook up."

"Darryl, Darryl." Zoey called out while walking his way.

As Zoey got a little closer, she saw Darryl lying on his stomach with a growing puddle of blood under him.

"Oh my God, Darryl, get up! Get up now, baby!" she screamed as she hurried to hold onto him.

Ms. Mathews rushed into the house to call the ambulance, hoping they could save him. Zoey cried and begged him not to leave her, but by the time the ambulance and police got there, it was too late. Darryl was pronounced dead on the scene. Ms. Mathews felt bad for how her daughter acted out over his death, but her tears were for Mya. With him being dead and gone, the chances of finding her were very slim.

◆

"What's your plan, nigga?" Jerome asked, passing Monsta a blunt.

Monsta smiled then hit his blunt. "A nigga finally free, and to be honest, all I wanna do is go home and see my mama. Being on bullshit, I fucked up with her bad. I need to fix that shit for real, man."

"You know I've been going to that shop and checking ol' boy out. He ain't even been there like that for real."

"It don't even matter, I might need you for something later. Can you handle another job?"

"You askin' too many questions, my boy. Drop that paper and whatever needs to be done, I got you."

Monsta stared at his mom's house for another second before climbing out of the car. He wasn't a bitch in no type of way, but this moment was very special to him. Walking in the house and seeing Mya sitting on his mama's lap, playing and laughing, almost made a real gangsta cry.

"Ma."

Ms. Caldwell jumped a little. "Damn, boy, you scared me. I'm telling you now, if you had somebody take her from her mama and then escaped, I'ma kill your crazy ass."

Monsta laughed while taking a seat next to her and Mya on the couch. "I got released."

Ms. Caldwell noticed how Mya had stopped playing just so she could stare at Monsta. She'd never seen him before, but for some reason, she wanted him. It's as if she knew who he was to her.

"Go ahead, boy, get her. I know you ain't even trying to be scared now."

Monsta slowly grabbed Mya. Ms. Caldwell got up to let him have some privacy. She could see he was emotional about finally meeting his baby girl.

"Hey, Mya, I'm yo' daddy."

Mya rested her head on his chest, and Monsta was grateful for that. Holding on to his baby girl, Monsta realized just how crazy he acted towards Sunshine. She had carried then pushed out his first and only child, and he needed to appreciate her for doing a great job while he was acting an ass.

As he rubbed Mya's back so she could fall asleep, he came up with a plan. He knew Sunshine was going crazy without her, and he didn't want her to suffer. He figured that maybe if he let her come get her, they could probably work out a schedule where he could get her from time to time. He didn't even care about sharing her with Jonas since he knew Sunshine won't make any moves without that nigga's say so. Monsta gave Mya a few kisses on her cheek as she slowly dozed off staring in his eyes.

"I love you so much. I promise I'ma act right, so I can be in your life."

Ms. Caldwell listened from the kitchen and knew deep down her son was telling his baby the truth. Although he just came home, his attitude was so different as if he really had matured.

"She is so beautiful, isn't she?" Ms. Caldwell asked as she walked back into the living room.

Monsta had a huge smile on his face. "Yeah, man. She looks just like Sunshine but got my eyes for sure."

"That baby looks like you, she's just yellow like her mama."

Monsta questioned her opinion. "You think so?"

"Hell yeah, boy," she replied.

Monsta sat there for a few minutes in complete silence. He needed to talk to Sunshine but didn't want to scare her or anything. He just wanted to apologize and go from there.

"Ma, can you call Sunshine for me?"

"Fuck no. Besides, that girl never gave me her number when I saw her in the market a few months ago."

Monsta reached in his pocket and pulled out the phone that he had while locked up. "I got her number."

"You call her then."

"Nah, you call her on your phone and get her over here. I don't want her to know I'm out yet. I got an idea, I just need you to help me."

Ms. Caldwell shook her head. "Alright, let me go get my phone."

Before giving her the number, Ms. Caldwell and Monsta went over the plan. From what she heard, it was a good plan. All they needed was for Sunshine to come over without an attitude.

"Hello."

They had her on speaker phone and could tell she'd been crying but only stopped long enough to answer the phone.

"Hey, Sunshine, this is Wendy. How are you?'

Sunshine's mind was everywhere and because of that, she never gave any thought to how she got her number.

"Hey."

"Look, can you come over? I would like to talk to you."

Sunshine didn't want to go over knowing the first thing she'd ask is where Mya was. On top of that, Jonas left with his brother and cousins to find Mya and asked her not to leave the house.

"I don't think that's a good idea."

"Please, I really need to speak with you. It's about Mya."

Sunshine jumped up. "What about her?" she asked, damn near yelling.

"Just get here," she demanded.

"I'll be over there in a few."

Soon as she stepped out of the shower, Sunshine saw that her mom and sister had been blowing her phone up.

"Fuck y'all, and y'all bitches better find my baby!" she yelled as she started to put her clothes on.

That shower woke her up, but now she was back to thinking about her baby. She needed to hold her baby and make sure she was alright. She then started to think that maybe Ms. Caldwell knew where Mya was.

"She just pulled up, Monsta."

Monsta picked up Mya and her car seat then disappeared in the room while his mama unlocked the door for Sunshine.

"Hey, come in, baby."

Sunshine slowly walked in and took a seat on the couch. "Hey, what did we need to talk about? What you got to say about my baby?"

Ms. Mathews didn't have to answer the question because Monsta walked into the room holding Mya.

"Damn, you still so fucking beautiful."

Sunshine jumped up hearing his voice. "Monsta, give me my fucking baby!" she yelled.

Monsta walked towards her. "Chill out. I just wanna talk to you. I swear I'm not on no bullshit."

"You kidnapped my fuckin' baby, that's all bullshit! Now hand her over!"

"I'm not trying to be on that shit. I really wanna work out our problems and make a schedule so I can come visit her. I'm willing to share her with your husband, I just wanna be in my daughter's life."

Sunshine wasn't trying to hear that shit. "You not her fuckin' daddy, now give me my baby!"

Ms. Caldwell shook her head knowing her saying that shit would push him overboard.

"Why the fuck you keep saying that bullshit? Look at her! Go ahead and look at her. That's my fuckin' baby!"

All the screaming made Mya cry.

"Please, Monsta, give me my baby. You got her crying, and she's scared. She needs her mama."

Ms. Caldwell finally got up. "Sunshine, my son is really trying to be in his child's life. By law, you can't just push him out of her life like that. He called you over so y'all can work shit out. He isn't even trying to fight with you."

"He kidnapped my fuckin' baby, so let's go ahead and get the law involved!" she snapped.

"See, bitch, I tried to be nice to you, and now you wanna bring the police in this. You need to be thanking me for getting her back. That nigga Darryl did this shit to blackmail me for some money, if you really wanna know the fuckin' truth."

"I just want my baby back."

"Can I at least get her every weekend?"

Sunshine couldn't believe he was serious about Mya spending time with his crazy ass. There's no way he was going to be in her life.

"Fuck no!"

"See, bitch, I tried to be nice, but you wanna talk shit to me and deny me my rights to be a father. You beggin' the bad guy to come out. You must miss me fuckin' you up, huh?"

Sunshine started digging in her purse for her phone, which only made Monsta nervous. He quickly snatched her purse from her.

"You not about to call nobody over here!" he yelled.

Ms. Caldwell saw this whole thing going left. It was clear there's only so much Monsta can take before he goes off.

"Just give her the baby and let them leave."

"No, fuck that shit."

With Mya still in his arms, Monsta stormed to his bedroom.

"Just leave, girl. He is pissed off. Leave now," Ms. Caldwell warned her.

"Are you fuckin' serious? I'm not leaving without my fuckin' baby."

Sunshine headed to his room to get Mya, but he met her at the door holding Mya in one hand and his gun in the other.

"No, Monsta, please don't hurt me," she said, backing up.

Monsta had an evil smirk on his face. "You wanna talk about my visitation rights now?"

Sunshine was scared and couldn't stop crying. All she could think about was him killing her and not being able to see her baby growing up.

"Boy, put that gun up!"

Monsta faced his mama. "Ma, take her upstairs with you. Me and her mama got some business to handle."

As she reached for Mya, Sunshine kept crying and begging Monsta not to hurt her.

"Monsta, you ain't got to do this. Please don't hurt me," she cried.

"I tried to be nice, but you like for a muthafucka to dog yo' ass."

Sunshine looked to Ms. Caldwell. "Please help me."

"Ma, I said take my baby upstairs, and don't be on no bullshit. I'd hate to have to hurt y'all in this muthafucka."

As she headed for the steps, Sunshine cried out, "Please don't leave me with him!"

Ms. Caldwell didn't want to leave her, but she didn't want any problems with her son. She ignored Sunshine's' cry for help and took the baby upstairs.

"Get your ass in the room!" he demanded.

Sunshine stood there shaking and crying. She was scared he was gonna kill her. She didn't move until he placed the gun back to her head.

"I don't wanna die, Monsta" she cried as she slowly entered the bedroom.

Monsta had her scared, in the corner. He started kissing her, making her very uncomfortable.

"Monsta, please."

"I was gonna let that nigga have you, but you had to fuck shit up. I only ever loved your ass, and you talk to me like I'm a bum nigga on the streets."

"I'm sorry, just please let me go home with my baby."

At this point, Monsta's free hand was roaming up her dress. Her tears couldn't stop the way his dick was growing and craving her at that moment.

"Take that shit off," he ordered.

"No, Monsta, please. You don't have to do this."

Monsta was no longer in the mood to talk. All he could think about was fucking her like he used to.

"You have been fuckin' that other nigga, now you wanna act like you too good for a nigga like me. Take that dress off and get your ass in the bed."

Not moving quick enough, Monsta slapped Sunshine down to the floor, then snatched her up by her hair and tossed her on the bed. She tried to kick him away from her, but that only made it easier to position himself between her legs.

Ms. Caldwell sat on the steps crying as she heard Sunshine scream out for help. She knew better than to stop what he was doing and figured Sunshine would be alright since this wasn't his first time doing this to her.

The whole time Monsta violated Sunshine, he whispered in her ear.

"I'm so sorry, baby. I really wanted us to work shit out."

The more she cried, the more he told her everything was her fault because she wouldn't hear him out about being in Mya's life.

Chapter 9

Jonas stopped by the house with Poppa to drop off food for Sunshine. He knew while Mya was still missing, she wasn't cooking. She barely wanted to eat.

"This girl is so fucking hardheaded. Before I left, I told her not to go anywhere."

Poppa shook his head. "Her baby missing, bro, she wasn't about to stay here while we were out searching. If anything, she's out looking too."

"You right, bro."

Jonas looked at his phone again as it went off. He quickly sent whoever to voicemail.

"Who was that?"

"My mother-in-law. I'm so pissed at them, I don't even wanna talk to them right now."

"Yeah, that was some foul shit going on over there."

Jonas' phone went off again. Thinking it was them calling again, he yelled into the phone without checking the caller ID. "What?"

"Jonas, it's me, Meka."

"My bad, cuz, what's wrong?" he questioned, hearing what he thought was crying.

Meka tried to calm down so she could explain to him what was going on.

"Meka, talk to me. Is it Mya?"

For some reason, those words rolled out first although he prayed her crying had nothing to do with his baby.

"No, Jonas, it's the shop. Somebody set it on fire and-"

"I'm on my way down there now."

Jonas didn't say anything, but Poppa knew to follow him out the door.

Pulling up to the strip, Jonas broke down seeing what he worked so hard for just gone.

"Damn, bro, what the fuck!" Poppa yelled, jumping out of the car.

Jonas was so hurt that he couldn't even get out of the car. His mind was all fucked up. First, he couldn't find Mya and felt like he failed as a father, and now his shop is gone.

Being numb, Jonas could barely talk to the investigators and the fire department. Lucky for him, Meka was there to save the day again, and tell them whatever they needed to know. The family stood around deep in their feelings as the firefighters fought to put the fire completely out. Afterwards, there were only bricks left on the outside. The inside was completely gone.

"What now?" Mason asked.

"Fuck this shit, man. I need to go find my baby," Jonas coldly said.

The family watched as he jumped back in the car and drove off.

"That nigga hurt, man."

"Hell yeah. Do y'all think we need to follow him home?" Meka asked.

Everyone looked at her. She's the one everyone followed on making decisions and now, they were stuck because she didn't have any answers.

Mason tossed Poppa his car keys. "Cuz, go check on your brother. Make sure that nigga ain't going home to end it all. I'm gonna ride with Meka."

Poppa jumped in the car to get to his brother.

Monsta sat up in the bed waiting for Jerome to call him back. After Sunshine cried herself to sleep, he went ahead and texted Jerome to fuck the shop up. At this point, Mr. Nice Guy was gone, and all that therapy bullshit didn't mean shit to him. Sunshine really did bring out the worst in him like he was told before.

"Aye, bitch, wake yo' ass up before I fuck you again."

Sunshine opened her eyes, looking around, not really remembering where she was.

"Wake yo' ass up and get the fuck out my fuckin' house!" he yelled.

This time, Sunshine jumped up. "Where is my baby, Monsta?"

"You know I loved the fuck out of you for real, and it's gonna take some time to get over you, but I can't fuck with you no more. I came home on some positive type shit. All I wanted was to come home and be a good daddy, but you wanna be on bullshit talkin' about Mya's not mine."

His words had Sunshine scared. She'd seen shows where the daddy killed the baby because of the mother. She started to cry again, praying this wasn't the case. She now regretted telling him he would never be Mya's father even though that's how she felt.

"Where's Mya?" she asked again.

Monsta laughed knowing she was scared. "You gon' get her back, bitch."

After Sunshine's dress was back on, Monsta grabbed her by the hair and dragged her out of his room.

"Monsta, that's enough. You had your fun for the day, now let her go home," Ms. Caldwell said, holding Mya.

Sunshine was crying, begging for Mya, but Ms. Caldwell wouldn't hand her over until Monsta said it was alright for her to do so.

"Monsta, if you want her to leave, you gotta let her have her baby back."

With tears in his eyes, he took Mya out of his mother's arms. "Mya, my baby girl, daddy loves you so fuckin' much, man. I'm sorry things didn't work out the way I wanted them to."

Monsta then placed a kiss on Mya's cheek before handing her over to Sunshine.

"Now hurry up and get out my house before I tie your ass up in the fucking basement."

Sunshine ran out the house so fast that she almost tripped holding Mya. She was so scared he would change his mind that Mya was still in her lap when she took off. She made it seven blocks away before she pulled over to just cry and thank God for making him set her free. She sat there crying her eyes out, trying to get her thoughts together and process exactly what the hell happened. After sitting there for what seemed like forever, Sunshine finally drove home. She wasn't sure what she was gonna tell Jonas, but Monsta had crossed the line and needed to pay.

Jonas was on the couch with a bottle. Poppa tried to get him to calm down when he got there, but he wasn't trying to hear shit.

"Bro, I can't sit here and watch you kill yourself. You gotta be stronger than that."

Jonas took another swig from the bottle. "I didn't ask you to come here. Look, just let me do me."

Poppa stood up, making Jonas feel like he was about to leave. To Jonas' surprise, he slapped the bottle out of his hand, causing it to fly across the room.

"You not about to do this shit to me, bro. We already lost pops from this shit. Are you trying to go out like him?"

Jonas could see the hurt in his eyes, but that didn't stop him from going after the bottle that was on the floor.

"Fuck that shit, bro!" Poppa yelled this time, trying to tackle Jonas down.

Jonas tried to fight back, but soon gave up. His mind went back to how his father's death affected everyone.

"Alright, man, let me go."

Sunshine rushed in the door holding Mya, causing the brothers to pause and stare at her. Jonas used whatever energy he had left to rush to them. Sunshine damn near fell in his arms.

"Jonas!" she cried.

She was crying so hard he could barely make out what she was trying to tell him.

"Calm down, Sunshine. Baby, I can't understand shit you're saying."

Sunshine felt sick just thinking about retelling her story. Jonas noticed she was getting sick and looked like she wanted to vomit. He grabbed Mya, handing her to Poppa. Racing up the stairs, Sunshine made it to the toilet just in time with Jonas right behind her. With her in a better light, Jonas was able to see that her face was swollen. That shit alone killed his buzz completely.

"What the fuck happened to you?"

Sunshine kept crying as she ran the water for a shower. "Can you please bathe Mya then put her in our bed?

"What the fuck happened and where the fuck did you find her?"

Sunshine snapped. "Jonas, please just give me a minute!"

"You know I don't like this shit, right?'

"Just a minute, please," she repeated.

Jonas went downstairs with Poppa. Mya was playing with her uncle, but it was clear she was tired. After a bath, he knew she would be knocked out.

"What's up with her?"

"I don't know, but I'm about to find out. Her face is all fucked up and shit, but she acts like she doesn't wanna talk about it right now."

Poppa didn't like that. "Man, she trippin'. Did she even tell you where Mya was?"

"Nah, she talkin' 'bout give her a minute."

Poppa shook his head. "Bro, your daughter was missing, and she came home fucked up with Mya in her arms. You gotta make her ass talk."

"Yeah, you right. I'll holla at you tomorrow, let me deal with my family."

"Nah, I'll be on the couch. I got a feeling you might need me."

Jonas was so clear minded. "Fuck you talking about, bro?"

"Go talk to your wife," Poppa said, laying on the couch.

Poppa knew something was about to jump off, and Jonas would need him. Jonas was the businessman of the family and would help anyone out, but he was also the muscle and never scared to pull the trigger, especially to protect the family.

After putting Mya in their bed, Jonas went to check on Sunshine. Hearing the shower water still going, he rushed into the bathroom.

"What the fuck, Sunsine?" Jonas yelled.

He saw his wife sitting in the shower with her legs pushed in her chest and her head down on her knees, crying her heart out. Her body trembled because the water had turned cold. Jonas cut the water off then wrapped her up in a towel.

"Come on, baby," he mumbled as he carried her back into the room.

As Sunshine laid in the bed, Jonas rubbed her back, hoping he could get her to calm down and talk to him. She wanted to tell him everything, but she was scared. It wasn't that she thought he couldn't deal with Monsta. It's because she knew he could and would do that shit. She knew Jonas would kill anyone that brought harm to her and Mya, and that's what scared her. She loved him and couldn't imagine him getting hurt or locked up behind her.

"Talk to me, baby. You gotta tell me what happened, please."

"She called saying she needed to talk about Mya. When I got there, Monsta was there playing with Mya," Sunshine cried.

"What? That nigga had my baby?" Jonas barked.

"I just wanted my baby back. I fought hard, and I'm just so sorry."

Jonas hugged Sunshine. "It's all good, baby, I'ma handle this shit."

Not wanting to hear anything else, Jonas grabbed his gun out of the closet before taking off down the stairs.

"Aye, bro, we need to roll out."

Poppa sat up, grabbing his gun off the table. He knew shit was about to go down and for that very reason, he didn't bother to take his shoes off or close his eyes.

"Let's go."

A while ago, when they were out and about, Sunshine had pointed out where Monsta and his mother stayed. While Jonas was telling him where they were going, Poppa was on his phone texting Mason. They were family and lived to ride for one another.

"I'm proud of you, Monsta. I'm surprised you let her go."

Monsta shook his head. "Man, shut the fuck up. I'm sick of her ass and you too. Instead of sitting in my face, you need to be getting the fuck out this house."

"Why am I leaving?"

"Why the fuck you think? I need you to leave just in case shit gets hot."

Ms. Caldwell didn't agree with her son. "Boy, bye. As much shit y'all been through, that girl ain't bringing no drama this way. Shit, she never did before."

Before walking away, Monsta mumbled, "This time might be different."

Monsta had never been the type to bitch up, so leaving his own shit wasn't an option. His mind was racing. Maybe Sunshine would pop up or maybe he was just being paranoid as hell. After gathering his thoughts, Monsta took out his phone to line his shit up just in case he needed the back up. Not too many knew he was out, and he wanted to keep it that way. With that being said, he texted Jerome.

Monsta: It might be something on the floor
Jerome: Let me know

While Monsta was in his bedroom trying to figure out if he had to kill somebody that night, his mother was on the phone telling her brother Dwayne to come get her.

"Do you know what time it is?" Dwayne yelled into the phone.

"Fuck all that! Some shit might pop off and I don't wanna be in the middle of all this bullshit," she tried to explain.

Dwayne sat up in his bed. "What the fuck you done got yourself into?"

"It wasn't me, Dwayne, now are you coming or not?"

"Oh hell nah, that boy back home? Don't tell me he's causing problems already, Wendy."

Shaking her head, she hung up the phone. She didn't have time to play with his ass.

Monsta got up to see her coming back downstairs. "Unc coming to get you?"

"Nah, he's on some bullshit. That muthafucka don't give a fuck about nobody but his fuckin' self."

"Fuck him. You should've let me fuck him up years ago, and he would've learned how to act right."

Ms. Caldwell stared at her son. He saw no wrong in the shit he said and did. "I really did pray they would get you some help while you were locked up. I don't see how they just let your crazy ass out."

"Bitch, I'm like this because of you. You got me all fucked up in the head and never wanted to get me help."

"Fuck you!"

"Fuck you too, bitch!" Monsta yelled back.

Not in the mood, she stormed outside. It was dark out, and she didn't have anywhere to go, so she stood on the porch smoking her cigarette.

"Whew! God, that little muthafucka in there gets on my fucking nerves so bad. Why did you give him to me?"

While his mother was outside smoking away her problems, Monsta went to lay down. With all the shit that was going on, all he could think about was how good Sunshine felt when he slid into her. He couldn't help but to laugh to himself knowing he was fresh out of jail and nutted in a bad bitch three times.

"That's still my baby," he mumbled.

Ms. Caldwell tossed her cigarette in the grass before turning around to go back in the house.

"Don't move, bitch. Move and I'll blow your fuckin' head off."

"Please, I swear it wasn't me," she cried.

Jonas slapped her in the head with his gun. "Shut the fuck up and open the door."

As she opened the door, Poppa gave her a warning.

"Don't scream or try anything stupid."

Ms. Caldwell was so scared, but for some reason, she did the complete opposite. As soon as they got in the house and shut the door she screamed.

"Monsta, help me!"

Monsta jumped up with his gun in his hand. He didn't give a fuck how he treated his mama, ain't no other nigga gonna hurt her as long as he was alive. He rushed out of the room busting off two shots before ducking back inside. Ms. Caldwell was smart enough to get down, but that didn't stop her from screaming out in fear. Monsta popped out again, shooting. Poppa and Jonas shot back, praying to hit his ass before he got them.

Monsta dipped off in the bedroom. He went straight to the closet to grab his other gun. Somebody was gonna die that night, and he'd be damn if it was him.

"Y'all muthafuckas better get the fuck out my house before the coroners be carrying y'all out!" he yelled.

"Come the fuck out, bitch ass nigga!" Jonas yelled.

Monsta started laughing. "Is that Jonas? The nigga that tried to take my boo boo from me."

Jonas couldn't believe how they were in the middle of trying to kill each other and this clown ass nigga was reciting movies and shit. Poppa was sick of the bullshit and knew if it came down to it, his brother would bitch up. He'd spent too much time trying to live right. Unlike Jonas, he loved that gun play shit. Without hesitation, Poppa put one shot in Ms. Caldwell's head.

"Bitch, come out now!"

Monsta ran out the room shooting wild at Jonas and Poppa, but never expected Mason to catch him slipping from the back. While they snuck in the front door with Ms. Caldwell, Mason snuck in the back just in case a muthafucka tried to escape. Everything worked. Seeing they had Monsta, down they ran out of the house untouched.

◆

Jonas peeked into the bedroom and saw Sunshine and Mya cuddled up in the bed. He was forever grateful he made it home to them. After a long, hot shower, he climbed in the bed with his family. Sunshine felt his warm body on hers then turned around to face him.

"I'm so sorry, baby. I didn't know all this was gonna happen."

Jonas placed a kiss on her swollen lips. "Shh… baby, don't worry about that shit. It wasn't your fault. Matter of fact, don't ever bring that nigga up."

"Jonas, I can't continue keeping secrets from you. I have to tell you something."

Hearing her cry alerted him. "Talk to me, baby. You don't ever have to be scared to tell me anything."

Sunshine hesitated to tell him about the rape at first, but the thought of not telling him and hurting him later made her open her mouth. "Jonas, Monsta raped me," she cried.

Jonas held her in his arms a little tighter as she cried. He felt bad as a husband for allowing that shit to happen.

"I'm so sorry, baby. I'm so sorry I wasn't there to protect you, but I promise that shit will never happen again."

Chapter 10

The next morning, Jonas and Sunshine cuddled in the bed watching the news. Although he needed to handle shit about the shop, he didn't want to leave her side. They listened as the reporter stated how the day before was the just first day of summer and so many crimes had been committed. That was how they both learned about Darryl.

"Damn, that's probably why they were calling all day."

"Yeah, they were calling me too, Jonas. I'm not sure if I'm ready to talk to them yet," Sunshine admitted.

"I'm on whatever tip you on, baby."

During that news segment, Sunshine also learned about the shop being burnt up.

"Oh my God, baby, I'm so sorry. Did you know about this?"

"I found out last night when the shit went down. I'm not as pissed as I was last night. I'm gonna use the insurance money to get me a new shop. With you and my family's support, I know this one will be bigger and better."

Sunshine gave him a kiss. "Can I work at the new shop?"

"Woman, are you crazy? No wife of mine is gonna be working," he said, laughing.

She also laughed. "Jonas."

Her beautiful smile is all he wanted to see after all she'd been through over the past few days.

"I was just playing. When you feel comfortable enough to have her in a daycare or something, it's whatever you want. I was waiting for you to bring that up."

Sunshine wanted to do something with her life, but the mention of daycare made her wonder if this is what she wanted.

"We'll see, baby."

After talking about the other latest news, they did a report on a house shooting on the eastside where the mother was found dead with one shot to the head with her son still fighting for his life after suffering several gunshot wounds. Jonas cut the TV off s pissed that Monsta wasn't dead. Sunshine had a bad feeling she knew who the report was about and by the change of Jonas' attitude, she knew he was also pissed.

"I still love you, baby, no matter what."

"I love you too."

Sunshine laughed feeling Mya climbing over her so she could squeeze between her mama and daddy.

"What's up, Mya Pie?"

Mya laughed, grabbing her daddy's beard. "Dada."

Jonas' face lit up. That was his first time hearing her call him that. Sunshine didn't say anything, but she heard Mya say it the day before when playing with Monsta. She couldn't crush him like that. That was a secret she would have to take to the grave.

The night of the shooting, Dwayne had a change of heart and went to go pick up his sister. He hated getting out of his bed so late, but she did sound like she was terrified. Besides, there's no telling with crazy ass Monsta running around. He knew there was a problem instantly when he pulled up to the front door wide open. He quickly called the police before walking in the door against the police's orders.

"Oh God no!" he screamed seeing his sister lying on the floor in a puddle of blood.

Dropping to his knees to hold and cry over his sister, he noticed Monsta's body laid out by the dining room.

"Monsta! Monsta!" he called out. Dwayne got up and raced over to his nephew.

"Monsta!"

To his surprise he was about to find a small faint pulse. Truth be told, he was pissed his sister was dead, and the devil himself was still breathing.

Monsta put up a long, hard fight in the hospital, but he won the battle. After being hit by eight bullets, he was alive, pissed and hurt about his mama, but alive. Once his few weeks were up, Monsta thought he was gonna get discharged then pop up at Sunshine's house for revenge, but the state had other plans for him. Detective Marshall was on the case and made sure to put him where he belonged. In prison. Finding his phone was all she needed seeing everything he did was in that very phone.

Once he was locked back up, Monsta tried that "he needed help" shit again, but they weren't having it. They were gonna make sure he did all of his time this go round. He thought that was bullshit. This time, he was traumatized because he'd witnessed the death of both of his parents and couldn't get revenge.

Monsta laid in his bed thinking about his mama. He was sad about the way shit went down with her, but he tried to warn her. He begged her to get out of the house that night. For a while, he put the blame on himself, but then it was clear it was his uncle's fault for not coming to pick her up earlier when she asked. It was easier for him to find a way to blame everyone except for himself. He still saw no wrong in his actions.

"At least I got a chance to hold my baby. No matter what, that's my fuckin' baby," he mumbled to himself.

Monsta was so caught up in talking to himself about Mya that he didn't see his new enemy sneaking up on him.

"What's up, nephew? I heard you were back," Big Rock coldly said.

Before Monsta could sit up or even speak, Big Rock stabbed him in the neck with his shank.

"That's for Rock, bitch."

Big Rock was already doing life and didn't give a fuck about nothing after losing his son not too long ago. Word got around that he was helping the state bring Monsta down, but everything went downhill and Monsta was set free. After they found Rock in the shower stabbed up, Big Rock knew he had to kill his own nephew.

Three Months Later

Sunshine stepped out of the shower still feeling sick to her stomach. "This shit can't be happening again."

Just an hour ago, she pulled out the brown bag she got from the pharmacy the day before. She knew deep down inside what the test was gonna say, but that was the least of her worries. Looking over her calendar for the last few weeks, Sunshine knew if she really was pregnant then she got pregnant around the time Monsta attacked her which was right after their vacation. Although she wasn't sure, she didn't feel right knowing the baby could be Monsta's. Just the thought of it made her sick again.

It took her forever to go back to the bathroom to check her test, but it had to be done. She sat on the bed with her towel wrapped around her, holding a positive pregnancy test with tears in her eyes. At this point, she wasn't sure if she even wanted to tell Jonas about the baby. She then thought about how they were working on being completely honest with each other. She couldn't just abort the baby without him knowing.

Jonas had just walked in from checking in on his new building. Everything was falling in place and in another month or so, the new shop will be up and running. He raced upstairs to tell his wife the good news.

"Hey, baby, what's up?"

Sunshine lifted her head, looking sad.

"I dropped Mya off with Meka, so you can get some extra rest. What's wrong? Why are you looking like that?" he questioned.

Sunshine sat there shaking, trying not to cry.

"Come on, baby, I told you to start talking to me. Good communication is the only way we can work out any problem."

"Jonas, I'm scared. I try to talk to you about everything, but I'm scared."

"Of what, baby?" he questions.

Sunshine passed him the test.

Jonas' face lit up. "You serious? This for real, Sunshine?" he asked, pulling her into a tight hug.

Sunshine loved the way he was excited about them having a baby, but she knew the news was gonna crush him.

"Why are you crying? This is great news, right?"

Sunshine pulled away from Jonas, crying. "Jonas, I'm so sorry."

"Fuck you sorry for? Talk to me now, Sunshine!" he yelled.

Sunshine kept crying, but it got Jonas to thinking.

"Aww hell nah! Are you fuckin' serious?

"Sorry. I'm so sorry, baby."

Although Jonas knew the back story and what went down, just the thought of her carrying a baby for Monsta broke his heart. He wasn't ready to face reality. He took off downstairs. He needed to get away from Sunshine before he said some shit he didn't mean.

Sunshine ran behind him, but he was long gone by the time she put on her clothes. Standing on the porch, Sunshine felt stupid for even telling him.

"So, you back on this shit, bro?"

Jonas laid across his couch drunk with an empty bottle on his chest. It had been three weeks since he spoke to Sunshine and loneliness was getting the best of him. He knew the rape wasn't her fault, but just the thought of the baby not being his made him hate Sunshine in a way. They had been fucking without a condom and nothing. But the first time Monsta got free and had his way with her, boom! A baby... maybe.

Poppa got the bottle from him and tossed it in the trash. Jonas was getting on his nerves. Here he was about to open up the new *Bentley's Cuts* in a few days, and he could barely get off the couch.

"I should beat his ass. What do you think, Poppa?" Mason asked.

"Nah, bro, gon' be good."

"Poppa, you my nigga and all, but I need to be honest with you. He's not gonna get better like this. When he gets in his feelings and shit not right with Sunshine, he drinks like this. Then they get back together, and he stops or whatever. I think we need to check him in so he can get clean for real. That's the only way, cuz. I love y'all and wouldn't tell you anything wrong."

Poppa sat there thinking about what Mason said and knew he was right.

"Can you help me look into this shit?"

"Hell yeah. Besides, I'm trying to get Nakia some help too. She is getting out of control."

Poppa called Sunshine over so they all could talk. By her being his wife, they wanted to run the idea with her.

"Hey, y'all, what's up," Sunshine said, walking in and greeting Poppa and Mason.

"We called you over here to talk to you about something important."

Sunshine was confused as she looked around for Jonas. It had been weeks, and she missed him. This meeting worried her.

"Where's Jonas?"

Poppa and Mason led her to the living room where Jonas was knocked out on the couch.

"Jonas, get up!" she yelled, shaking him a little.

"He's not gonna get up."

Sunshine turned to Poppa. "What are you talking about?" she asked, touching his chest to make sure he was still breathing.

Mason tried to jump straight to the point. "Have a seat, we wanna talk to you about saving Jonas."

"What's wrong with him?"

Poppa shook his head. He forgot he never told her about his secret all this time. Once Sunshine was comfortable on the couch, they told her about his past with abusing alcohol and how he had relapsed again and had been on and off for the last few months.

Sunshine was speechless. She had no idea that on top of her bullshit, he was battling his own demons. She stopped crying long enough for them to tell her about a rehab he could enter so he could get the proper help he needed. Although she was all for it, something in her still wanted to talk to him first.

After Mason and Poppa left, Sunshine stayed at his apartment and cleaned up for him. She couldn't believe how he was really living. It was crazy how most of the bottles were in the living room as if he never made it to any other room in the apartment.

"Where my shit at?" Jonas mumbled in a grouchy, drunk voice.

Sunshine walked into the living room. "All that shit is gone, Jonas."

"What you doin' here? Who let you in?"

She took a seat on the couch next to him. "Your family told me what was going on with you and they want me to have you sign some papers so you can get into rehab. What do you think about that?"

"Fuck I need rehab for? I don't have a fuckin' problem, and I'm not going nowhere."

"Jonas, we have a baby on the way. You gotta be sober to help raise it."

Jonas didn't say anything. The last thing he wanted to do is think about Sunshine carrying Monsta's baby. He stood up, barely making it to the kitchen. Sunshine followed him and watched him search around for another bottle.

"You are too much of a man to go out like this, baby. Listen, I know you're upset about there being a chance this is Monsta's baby, but Mya is his for sure and you love the fuck out of her."

"That's not it, Sunshine."

"What is it then Jonas? If it's not about me being pregnant with this baby, what is the problem?" she questioned.

"I love you and Mya, and I know I will love the baby you're carrying. When you first told me you were pregnant and I figured out what you were scared to tell me, to be honest, my feelings were hurt. What had me fucked up is how I handled the situation. I ran out on you like I wasn't a man and yet, here you go, making sure I'm alright."

Sunshine grabbed his hand. "We both have some issues we need to work on, but as long as we have each other and support and love one another, everything will be alright."

Jonas leaned over to give her a kiss. "I love you so much, baby."

Sunshine smiled as he rubbed on her little stomach. "I love you too, and we're gonna get through whatever."

Jonas and Sunshine chilled and talked about their future with another baby. They decided to keep the rape and the possibility of Monsta being the father a secret. Not that it was anyone else's business.

"Hold up, baby," Jonas said, getting up from the couch so he could answer the door.

Meka, Poppa, Mason and Nakia walked in carrying Mya and food.

"What are y'all doing here?"

"Surprise cousin night," Meka said, handing Mya over to Jonas.

Jonas placed a kiss on Mya's cheek. "What's up, baby girl? Daddy missed you so much."

Mya was all smiles as she pulled on his beard. That was her way of showing him love.

Everyone was eating, talking and having a good time but Nakia.

"It's boring, where the drinks at?"

"Chill out, sis, we ain't on that shit tonight," Mason told her.

Nakia rolled her eyes. "So, I can't drink 'because Jonas has a problem? That's really fucked up."

Sunshine started to say something, but Meka beat her to it.

"Shut up, girl. You have a problem too and the sooner you accept it, the sooner we can get you help."

"I don't have a fuckin' problem," Nakia said, getting up.

Poppa was getting irritated. "Tonight, we wanted to come together as a family so we could help each other. Me and Jonas lost our father due to him abusing alcohol, and I think if we stick together and support each other, we can make sure no one ends up like my daddy.

Jonas stared at the ground. He felt like all eyes were on him, but he understood where his brother was coming from. "I've been hiding what I was from my beautiful wife up until today. Still buzzed a little, I promised her I would get all the help I could. We are expecting another baby in a few months, so I need to be here, and in the right state of mind to help raise my family."

"Aww! Congratulations to you two," Meka said with a huge smile on her face.

It seemed as if everyone was happy but Nakia.

"That ain't got shit to do with me. I don't have a fuckin' problem like Jonas."

"We both have a problem. The only difference is I know and wanna get help while you're still in denial. Let them help you too."

"Fuck all y'all. This bitch done came in this family acting like she Miss Goodie Two Shoes and now y'all wanna point out people's flaws. Fuck her too. She not even in our family for real."

Sunshine jumped up. "What's the problem?"

"Bitch, you the problem. It was always you, bitch. Jonas didn't relapse until he got with your toxic ass."

Jonas tried to stand in the middle of them to prevent a fight, but when Nakia tried to swing, Sunshine went crazy. For the simple fact that she got her ass beat by Kyrah, she made sure to fuck Nakia up, showing her she wasn't the one to play with. Everyone tried pulling Sunshine off Nakia, but her little ass had turned into The Hulk and had no much strength that made it harder.

After finally getting them apart, Nakia started yelling. "Y'all supposed to be my fuckin' family and y'all stay takin' this bitch's side. Did y'all forget her real baby daddy killed my fuckin' brother?"

"Nakia, we ain't forgotten shit, but that nigga got what he deserved," Mason replied.

"Fuck that! Monsta only got dealt with when it came to that bitch and her baby!" she yelled.

Meka sat Mya back down since she was no longer crying. "Nakia, all that shit is in the fuckin' past. We are all family now and need to move forward."

"Fuck y'all!" Nakia yelled, storming out the door, making sure to slam it behind her.

The apartment was quiet for a while. Everyone was in their own thoughts.

"Sunshine, I don't care how Nakia feels about you. You my fucking sister, and I think you good for my brother," Poppa admitted.

After that, everyone else spoke out on how much they loved Sunshine and Mya. Come to find out, only Nakia had a problem with her.

Soon, everyone headed out, leaving Sunshine there with Jonas and Mya. It was late and she decided to stay there with Jonas.

"If you check yourself in, what are you gonna do about the opening of the new shop?"

"Meka's gonna help out like she's been doing. I don't want to hold up the opening, but I know I need help. I have to be strong for everyone."

"We're all gonna be strong for you too, baby."

Jonas gave his wife a kiss before they both dozed off. Everything was looking up for them.

Let's Chat

*Email your answers to
Messiah.nf@gmail.com*

Do you think Sunshine will ever be able to build another relationship between her mom and sister? What reasons do you have to support your reason?

Do you think Nakia should have blamed her Brother Trevor's death on Sunshine? What reasons do you have to support your reason?

Do you think Kyrah should have blamed her Brother Lamar's death on Sunshine? What reasons do you have to support your reason?

Do you think if Monsta was given the chance he would have been a great father to Mya? What reasons do you have to support your reason?

Was Sunshine the problem all along? What reasons do you have to support your reason?

Was you surprised that Darryl was the one working with Monsta? What reasons do you have to support your reason?

Do you think Poppa was wrong for killing Ms. Caldwell? What reasons do you have to support your reason?

Do you think Sunshine and Jonas will make it? What reasons do you have to support your reason?

Do you think Nakia had her reasons for hating Sunshine so much? What reasons do you have to support your reason?

T. Friday was born and raised in Detroit, Michigan. At the age of 36, she is the mother of five children. Three handsome boys ages 19, 15, and 13, and two beautiful girls ages 9 and 8.

At a very early age, T. Friday fell in love with reading books such as *Babysitters Club*, *Sweet Valley High* and *Goosebumps* books by R.L Stine. It wasn't until she was in her early teens that she was introduced to Urban Fiction books. That's when she knew she wanted a career in the book industry.

January of 2016, T. Friday had her left leg amputated and that's when she realized she had been taking her life for granted, and it was time to make her dreams come true. She picked up a pen and paper then started writing. In May of 2017, T. Friday signed her first contract with Racquel Williams who is the owner of RWP.

Now, in 2021 she is the author of 25 books. She has plans to continue writing until one day all of her books are turned into movies.

T. Friday's Book Catalog

Intrigued by a Savage's Love (Standalone)

Finding Love in a Real Boss 1

Finding Love in a Real Boss 2

Nasir & Kennedy: Luv in the Gutta (Standalone)

In Love with a Street Princess (Standalone)

To Be Loved by a Brick Boy 1

To Be Loved by a Brick Boy 2

To Be Loved by a Brick Boy 3

Yearnin' for the Love of a Thug (Standalone)

All Cried Out: Lovin' a Detroit Nigga 1

All Cried Out: Lovin' a Detroit Nigga 2

When Love Calls the Shots (Standalone)

Saving all my Love for a Young Boss 1

Saving all my Love for a Young Boss 2

Jewel and Javarri: His Love Wasn't Enough (Standalone)

Tears Shed from Loving a Trap Nigga 1

Tears Shed from Loving a Trap Nigga 2

A Detroit Nigga Finessed my Love (Standalone)

Pretty Bitches get Even (Standalone)

Aaliyah & Marcel: Side Chicks Wanna Be Loved Too (Standalone)

Prettier in Pink (Standalone)

Boo'd up with a Young Outlaw for Christmas

When a Street King Wants You

Upgraded to a Real Boss

Upgraded to a Real Boss 2

Author's Contact Information

 Author T Friday

 Authortfriday

 @TFriday9

 Messiah.nf@gmail.com

If you haven't already, sign up for my email blast for new updates on all my books.

ALL MY BOOKS CAN BE FOUND ON AMAZON.COM

Read a book, leave a review on Amazon or Goodreads, and tell a friend.

www.ingramcontent.com/pod-product-compliance
Lightning Source LLC
Chambersburg PA
CBHW071945150726
47999CB00001B/307